GOLD COAST ANGELS

The hottest docs, the warmest hearts, the highest drama

Gold Coast City Hospital is located right in Australia's Surfers Paradise, at the heart of the Gold Coast, just a stone's throw away from the world famous beach.
The hospital has a reputation for some of the finest doctors in their field, kind-hearted nurses and cutting-edge treatments.

With their 'work hard and play hard' motto, the staff form a warm, vibrant community where rumours, passion and drama are never far away.
Especially when there is a new arrival—fresh from Angel Mendez Hospital, NYC!

When utterly gorgeous bad-boy-with-a-heart Cade rolls into town, trouble is definitely coming to Surfers Paradise!

If you loved **NYC Angels**, you'll love the high drama and passion of this irresistible four-book Mills & Boon® Medical Romance™ series!

**GOLD COAST ANGELS:
A DOCTOR'S REDEMPTION**
by Marion Lennox

is also available this month

Dear Reader

I've loved being a part of the *Gold Coast Angels* series, and can't wait to catch up with all the amazing people who work there.

My heroine, Lucy, is ready to take on the world. She's a dedicated midwife, of course, and loves her job—until she finds out she is going to be a single mother with twins.

Without support of family, Lucy would be finding it even tougher without the warmth and caring of her work friends—and that's where Gold Coast City Hospital comes into its own.

But it's gorgeous Dr Nikolai Kefes who really takes her under his gorgeous wing (those shoulders...!), and Lucy discovers that she's not the only person who has someone special missing in her life. Can she heal Nikolai's past hurts and make this wonderfully caring doctor love again?

I hope you have as much fun as I did with Nick and Lucy's love life—enjoy the *Gold Coast Angels* series.

Warmest wishes

Fiona McArthur

GOLD COAST ANGELS: TWO TINY HEARTBEATS

BY
FIONA McARTHUR

MILLS & BOON

Dedicated to my cousin John, who is toughing it out,
so proud of you, and to Aunty Yvonne, Lee, who is also awesome,
Gay and Eveline.

First published in Great Britain 2013
by Mills & Boon, an imprint of Harlequin (UK) Limited.
Harlequin (UK) Limited, Eton House, 18-24 Paradise Road,
Richmond, Surrey TW9 1SR

© Harlequin Books S.A. 2013

Special thanks and acknowledgement are given to Fiona McArthur
for her contribution to the *Gold Coast Angels* series

ISBN: 978 0 263 23380 3

Harlequin (UK) policy is to use papers that are natural, renewable
and recyclable products and made from wood grown in sustainable
forests. The logging and manufacturing process conform to the
legal environmental regulations of the country of origin.

Printed and bound in Great Britain
by CPI Antony Rowe, Chippenham, Wiltshire

Mother to five sons, **Fiona McArthur** is an Australian midwife who loves to write. Medical Romance™ gives Fiona the scope to write about all the wonderful aspects of adventure, romance, medicine and midwifery that she feels so passionate about—as well as an excuse to travel! Now that her boys are older, Fiona and her husband, Ian, are off to meet new people, see new places, and have wonderful adventures. Fiona's website is at www.fionamcarthur.com

GOLD COAST ANGELS

The hottest docs, the warmest hearts, the highest drama

This month, sexy lone wolf Sam is given a second chance
at life by bubbly nurse Zoe in
A DOCTOR'S REDEMPTION by Marion Lennox

And midwife Lucy's first day at work
takes an unexpected turn when gorgeous new colleague Nick
suggests she takes a pregnancy test in
TWO TINY HEARTBEATS by Fiona McArthur

Then, in November, nurse Chloe falls for brooding surgeon
and single dad Luke in
BUNDLE OF TROUBLE by Fiona Lowe

While Cade and Callie can't get that steamy one-night stand
out of their minds in
HOW TO RESIST TEMPTATION by Amy Andrews

Don't miss this fabulous four-book series full of breathtaking
drama, heartwrenching emotion and sizzling passion!

**These books are also available in eBook format
from www.millsandboon.co.uk**

CHAPTER ONE

LUCY PALMER WAS so excited even the ride up in the lift made her feel queasy. She'd thought she'd grown out of that.

Today, officially, she could say she was a part of the state-of-the-art Gold Coast City Hospital and she'd done it all herself. Her excitement had been building since graduation fourteen weeks ago.

This wasn't just three years of hard study and unpaid practical placements, this was the start of a mission she'd lived and breathed for ever.

Lucy couldn't wait to be allocated her first birth suite caseload because she was going to be the best midwifery grad they'd ever seen.

The midwifery floor manager, Flora May, ex-air force medic with a gruff voice and, Lucy suspected, a well-camouflaged heart of gold, had met Lucy in one of her placements during her training. Flora's assessment of Lucy's aptitude for the profession had helped very much in her successful interview and Lucy couldn't have asked for a better role model than Flora.

As the orientation tour ended Flora snapped her heels together and waved to the busy floor. Unexpectedly her angular face changed and she smiled with genuine warmth.

'And welcome, Palmer. I've given you Monday to Friday shifts for the first month, so I'll be here if you need advice.'

A friendly face while she settled in. Lucy decided that sounded blissful. 'Thank you.'

'Hmph.' Sentiment should be set aside, obviously, Lucy thought with an internal smile as Flora went on. 'Take Sally Smith, she's a teen mum admitted for threatened premature labour at thirty-three weeks. She needs someone she can relate to.'

This was accompanied by a dry look. 'Night staff will give you Sally's handover in birth suite one.' Flora raised an eyebrow. 'You'll be fine. Let me know if you need help and I'll be your wing man. Any questions, find me.'

The boss would be her wing man? Lucy grinned at the funny wordage and resisted the urge to salute.

Flora marched off and Lucy felt for the first time that someone other than her fellow ex-students was willing to believe she had the makings of a good midwife.

It would have been nice if her mother had been supportive instead of bitter and twisted, but she wasn't going there because nothing was going to spoil this day. Or her confidence, because Flora believed she could do this well.

Her stomach fluttered uncomfortably again and she sucked in a breath. Forget nerves, this was what she'd been born for.

When she knocked and entered the first birth suite and the night midwife didn't look up from writing her notes, Lucy faltered, felt tempted to cough or go back and knock again, but she didn't.

The pale young woman lying curled on her side blinked so Lucy stepped just inside the door and smiled, but the girl on the bed rolled her eyes, and then looked away before shutting them. Tough room, Lucy thought ruefully before, with another deep breath, she crossed to the bed.

The night midwife still didn't look up, so Lucy passed her by and smiled at her patient as she tried to imagine what it would be like to be seventeen, pregnant, and now scared her baby would be born prematurely, in a place where she knew no one.

'Hello, Sally, I'm Lucy. I'll be looking after you today when your night midwife goes home.' Lucy glanced around the otherwise empty room, and no boyfriend or mother was tucked into any corner she could see. Maybe Sally's mother had trained in the same school as hers, Lucy thought, and she knew how that felt. Lack of family support was not fun at all.

The young mum-to-be opened her eyes briefly, nodded, and then rolled carefully over onto her other side, stretching the leads that held the monitor on her stomach.

Really tough room, Lucy thought with a gulp.

Finally the night midwife put down her pen and looked across. 'I'm Cass. I've just done my fifth night shift and can't wait to get out of here.'

Lucy blinked and glanced at Sally's rigid back. Not a very nice intro, she thought, or what Lucy expected from a hospital she'd only ever heard praise about.

To make it worse, Cass didn't look at anything except her notes or, occasionally, the graph of contractions on the machine. 'So this is Sally, seventeen, thirty-three weeks, first baby, and has had intermittent back pain since three this morning. No loss on the pad she's wearing and the CTG is picking up the contractions as five-minutely.'

The lack of emotion sat strangely in a room where emotion was usually a big factor and Lucy began to suspect why Flora May had sent her in here. Lucy wanted to care for Sally, not treat her like an insect in a jar.

Cass sighed as if the story would never end and Lucy wished the midwife would just go home and let her read the notes herself. But of course she couldn't say that, especially on her first day. But she was feeling less timid by the second. Something she'd discovered inside herself when she'd discovered midwifery.

Then Cass went one worse. 'The foetal fibrinectin test for prem labour couldn't be done because she's had sex in the last twenty-four hours.'

Brutal. Lucy saw Sally's shoulder stiffen and winced in sympathy for the callousness of a clinical handover that lacked sensitivity. Lucy vowed she'd never be like this. And now she seriously wished the other midwife gone.

Cass certainly didn't notice and went on in the same bored tone as she read from her notes. 'No urinary symptoms or discharge but we've sent swabs and urine away for microscopy.'

Okay, Lucy understood that she needed to know it had been done, because infection was the most common reason for early labour and miscarriage.

Cass went on. 'She's had three doses of oral tocolytic, which has slowed the contractions, been started on antibiotics four-hourly, and the foetal heart trace...' She glanced at the long strip of paper cascading from the monitor that evaluated baby heart rate and uterine contractions without looking at the patient. Lucy hated impersonal technology. It was too easy for staff to look more at machines than the patient.

Cass shrugged. 'I think she's more stable than when

she arrived. First dose of steroids was given at three-thirty a.m., so she's due another that time tomorrow morning, if she's still here.'

Cass looked up. 'Any questions?'

No way did she want to prolong Cass's stay. Where did you *not* learn your people skills? Lucy thought, but instead she asked, 'What time did the doctor last see Sally?'

'It's all in the notes.' Cass glanced down. 'The registrar at four a.m., but her obstetrician, Dr Kefes...' For the first time some emotion heightened the colour on Cass's face and she looked almost feline. 'Nikolai's delicious.' She sighed as if he was there in front of her and Lucy cringed.

'Nikolai will see her at rounds this morning. He's always punctual at eight so be ready. I'm off.' She snapped shut the folder and uncoiled herself from the chair. 'Bye, Sally.' She handed the folder to Lucy and left without waiting for her patient's reply.

Lucy frowned at the door as it shut, decided even the mention of the doctor as delicious was unprofessional, glanced around for inspiration on winning Sally's confidence after the nurse from hell had departed, and set about changing the dynamics of the room.

She spotted a little black four-wheeled stool and pulled it around to the other side of the bed to see her patient's face before sitting down.

The stool brought her not too close but just under the level of Sally's eyes so she wasn't crowding or looking down at her. After a few moments Sally opened her eyes. 'So how are you feeling, Sally?'

'Crap.'

Lucy smiled. Succinct. 'Fair enough. Can you be

more specific? Your back?' Sally nodded and Lucy continued, 'Worse or better than when you came in?'

'A lot worse.' Sally blinked suspiciously shiny eyes and Lucy wanted to hug her. Instead, she considered their options.

'Okay, that's not good. Let's sort that first. I'll take the monitor off for a few minutes while I check your observations, and have a little feel of your tummy before we put the belts back on more comfortably. Then we'll see if we can relieve some of the discomfort.'

Lucy glanced at the little watch that her friends had all pitched in for her on graduation. Pretty and practical, like her, they'd said, and she still winced because they'd known her mother wouldn't show for the event and she'd be disappointed.

That might even have been why she'd made that dumb choice with Mark after one too many unfamiliar mojitos, but it had been nice to bask in appreciation for a change.

She shook off regrets because they were a waste of time. She'd learnt that one the hard way by watching her mother.

Seven-thirty a.m., so she had half an hour before the obstetrician arrived to assess her patient's condition. Lucy wanted an overall picture of Sally's general health and mental state before then. But mostly she wanted Sally to feel comfortable with her so she could best represent her concerns when more new caregivers arrived. She'd better get started.

Nikolai Kefes, Senior Obstetrician at Gold Coast City Hospital, discreetly named Adonis by his female colleagues, had a strong work ethic. Seventy per cent of his life centred on work, twenty per cent went to his sister, Chloe, and the other ten per cent was divided equally between sport and brief affairs with sophisticated women.

Nick hated being late for ward rounds but there was no way he could have ignored the distress call from his sister, and by the time he'd parked his car at the hospital it was half an hour after he'd expected to start.

Chloe worried him. She had worried him since she was sixteen and in more trouble than he could have imagined, so much so that she'd changed both their lives. But he could never regret giving her the support she needed when she needed it.

Not that she'd always appreciated his attempts to shield her from the hardships that arose when two young people were suddenly cast out in the world without a penny. He still cringed to think how she would have survived if he hadn't followed her.

It was a shame their parents hadn't felt the same, but he'd given up trying to fathom them years ago.

But this morning Chloe had been adamant she would do things her way, despite this last disastrous relationship, and he wished she'd just swim to the surface and avoid becoming involved for a while.

He could only be glad he was in control of his own brief affairs. Short and sweet was not just a concept, more like a mantra for his life, because emotion was best left out of it. That way nobody got hurt.

The lift doors opened and he stepped out on the maternity floor. His eyes narrowed as he noted the arrival of his registrar at the nurses' station just ahead of him. If he wasn't mistaken, Simon had got dressed in a hurry, because his shirt showed the inside seams and the shadow of a pocket.

He guessed he should be thankful the majority of

his own nights were left undisturbed at this stage of his career, so he smiled, and cleared his mind of everything but his work. The familiar focus settled over him and his shoulders relaxed as he zeroed in on his junior.

'So, Simon. Tell me what's happening this morning.' He paused, looked him up and down and smiled. 'Then perhaps you could retire into the staffroom and turn your shirt the other way?'

Eight thirty-five a.m. In the past fifteen minutes Lucy had decided Sophie would definitely have her baby today. Around eight-fifteen the contractions had become strong and regular and Lucy had slipped out and rung the registrar because the eight a.m. arrival of the consultant hadn't occurred.

Neither had the arrival of the registrar, Lucy fumed, and twenty minutes' time lag wasn't good enough. She wasn't happy as she looked for Flora May again to let her know her patient still hadn't been seen.

Instead, she saw a tall, very athletic-looking man arrive at the desk, his immaculate suit dark like his short wavy hair, but it was his air of command that convinced Lucy he could be the person she expected. She diligently ignored the fact he was probably the most handsome man she'd ever seen and that maybe the horrible night midwife hadn't been far off.

'Dr Kefes?'

Both men turned to face her but she went straight for the one who obviously held the power.

'Yes?' His voice was low with a husky trace of an accent that was delightfully melodious, Mediterranean most likely, but she'd think about that later when she had a chance.

'I'm sorry to interrupt. I'm the midwife looking after

Sally Hill. She's seventeen years old and thirty-three weeks gestation in prem labour. I believe she's establishing active labour as we speak and you need to see her now.' She handed him the notes and said over her shoulder, 'This way, please.'

As he opened the notes and followed, Nikolai wondered briefly why he had allowed himself to be steered so determinedly when he usually had handover by his registrar and then did his rounds.

Of course, the young midwife seemed concerned, so that was a good reason, and she had made it difficult for him to refuse, he thought with an internal smile as he watched her reddish-brown ponytail swing in front of him.

He was more used to deference and suggestion than downright direction, but this day had started unusually, and it seemed it was going to proceed that way.

Ten minutes later Lucy stood beside the bed as she watched Dr Kefes and the respectful way he talked to Sally, and she could feel the ease of the tension in her own shoulders.

Thankfully, he was totally opposite from the way the night midwife had been. This tall man with the accent seemed genuinely empathetic with the young mum's concerns and symptoms. Even the tricky business of the physical examination was conducted with delicacy and tact.

Afterwards Nikolai removed his gloves and washed his hands then came back to the bed, where Lucy had helped Sally to sit up more comfortably. The two young women watched his face anxiously.

Dr Kefes smiled. 'It seems your baby has decided to have a birthday today. You are more than half-dilated and we will let the special care nursery know to expect a new arrival.'

Sally's face whitened and the first real fear showed in her eyes. He sat down on Lucy's stool and smiled gently at the young mum. 'This is a shock to you?'

Sally nodded but didn't speak. Lucy could see her lip trembling and she reached across and put her hand out. To her relief Sally grabbed her fingers and clung on while the doctor addressed her fears.

'You are in a safe place. Your baby is in a safe place. If you are worried, listen to your midwife.' He gestured at Lucy. 'This one, who was so determined I would see you first she practically dragged me in here before my round began.'

He smiled at Lucy and she could feel her cheeks warm with embarrassment, and something else, like pleasure that this gorgeous man had complimented her on her advocacy. But the best result was that Sally smiled as well.

He went on. 'We will all work towards this being a very special day for you and your baby.' He stood up. 'Okay?'

Sally nodded, and Lucy could tell she wasn't the only person in the room who had decided Nikolai Kefes was a man to put your faith in.

And Sally's birthing was special. Her baby was born three hours later. Dr Kefes was gentle and patient, and Sally was focused and determined to remain in control.

Lucy had borrowed the ward camera and captured some beautifully touching shots soon after the birth, because the neonatal staff were there for the baby, Dr Kefes managed the actual delivery, Flora May unobtrusively supervised, and she didn't have much to do herself.

The stylish bob of the neonatal specialist, Dr Callie Richards, swung as she paused and spoke to Sally while her staff wheeled tiny Zac out the door on the open crib towards the NICU. 'I think he'll be promoted to the special care nursery very quickly, but we'll check him out first in the NICU.'

Her eyes softened. 'You come and visit him as soon as you're up to it or I'll come to see you if he misbehaves before then.' Her gentle voice was warm and compassionate and Sally nodded mutely. Her eyes met Lucy's as her baby was wheeled away.

'He'll be fine,' Lucy whispered. 'He looks little but very strong.'

Sally sniffed and nodded and Lucy squeezed her hand. 'Let's get you sorted so you can go and see what he's up to.'

Afterwards, when Sally had showered and the two young women had had a chance to look at the photos, Lucy was very glad she'd taken them.

The luminous joy on Sally's face as she gazed at her tiny son—a close-up of a starfish hand, a tiny foot lying on his mother's fingers, and one of him snuggled against his mother's breasts before he'd been whisked away to the neonatal nursery, were all a comfort to a new mother whose baby had been taken for care somewhere else.

Even on the poor-quality prints in black and white that Lucy printed out on the ward computer Sally looked a beautiful mum.

As she waited in the wheelchair, Sally's finger traced the distinguishing features of her tiny son's face and body on the images.

'I'm glad I had you looking after me.'

Lucy squeezed Sally's shoulder. 'I'm glad I was here. Thank you for letting me share your birth.'

Her first birth as a proper midwife had been as empowering for Sally as she could make it. And she could tell that the young mum was pretty chuffed at how she'd managed everything that had been asked of her.

Lucy had never felt so proud of anyone as she was of Sally. She glanced around to see that they had collected everything from the room and pushed the chair forward. 'We'll drop this stuff in your room and then we'll go and see this gorgeous son of yours.'

Five hours later, at the end of the shift, a shift that had held her first prem birth, a quick catch of another impatient baby keen to arrive before the rest of the staff were ready, and a smile from a very senior obstetrician for a job well done, Lucy picked up her bag from the staffroom.

She should be feeling ecstatic as she walked past the sluice room on the way out but, in fact, she felt dreadful.

The nausea that had been building all day suddenly rushed up her throat in an imminent threat—so much so that she had to launch herself at the sluice-room sink in desperation.

Nikolai, too, was on his way out the door when he saw the sudden acceleration of the new midwife who'd been so diligent today.

He frowned as he realised the nature of her distress, and glanced hopefully left and right for someone else in scrubs, but saw nobody he could call on to assist her. He sighed, shrugged, and approached the doorway.

'Are you okay?' By the time he reached her it seemed it was over.

Her forehead rested on the tips of the fingers of one hand as she rinsed the sink. The fragility of her pale neck made him reach for his handkerchief and he leaned past her and dampened it under the cold running water. He wrung it out before handing it to her to wipe her face.

To his amusement she was so intent on patting her hot cheeks that she muttered thanks without turning. Later, perhaps it would be different, but at the moment it seemed she was just glad she'd made it to somewhere manageable.

Then she glanced back and he saw her glance hesitantly past him and he wondered if she expected the whole staff to be lined outside, watching her.

'Nobody else saw.'

Her shoulders sank with relief and he bit back a smile. So transparent.

'Thank goodness. It's crazy.' He could just catch the words because she seemed to be talking to his tie. 'I've been feeling nauseated all day and it just caught up with me.'

'Not pregnant, are you?' He smiled, in no way expecting the startled look of shock that spread over her face as she glanced up at him. Oh, dear me, Nikolai thought, and couldn't help flashing back to his sister all those years ago.

No doubt it was that connection that caused his sudden surge of protective feeling towards this wilting poppy in front of him, but the sudden urge to hug her disconcerted him. He hadn't wanted to drop a bombshell like that, neither had he had any intention of ruining her day, but it was far too late now. He resigned himself to waiting for her to gather herself.

'I can't be.' But even in that tiny whisper Nick heard the thread of perhaps. Perhaps. Perhaps?

She lifted her gaze to his again and he could see the intriguing green flecks in the hugeness of her horrified hazel eyes.

He'd put his foot in it, obviously. 'So you haven't tested for pregnancy?'

'Hadn't given it a thought,' she mumbled, and blushed. 'I didn't consider that precautions might let me down during my first and only ever one-night stand. And that was ages ago.' Her bitterness was unmistakable. She leant back over the sink to cover her face.

Nick winced at the vagaries of fate. Here was a woman anything but pleased by her fertility, while his sister would give anything to be able to fall pregnant again.

He didn't know how he could help, or even why he wanted to, but he couldn't just leave.

Maybe he was wrong. He knew nothing about her. 'Perhaps you're not pregnant. Could be gastro. Lack of food. You could try a pregnancy test. I have some in my rooms. Might even be negative.'

She looked at him, he saw the brief flare of hope, and she nodded. 'That seems sensible. Of course I'm not...' She blushed, no doubt at the blurting out of the indiscreet information she'd given him. He'd have liked to have been able to reassure her he could forget her indiscretion—no problem—but he wasn't sure how.

She didn't meet his eyes. 'It could just be the excitement of the day. Would you mind?'

'It's the least I can do after scaring you like that.' He smiled encouragingly and after a brief glance she smiled back tentatively. 'Follow me.'

He glanced sideways and realised she'd had to skip a little to keep up. He guessed he did take big steps compared to hers, and slowed his pace. 'Sorry.' He smiled down at her. 'It's been a busy day and I'm still hyped.'

Lucy slowed with relief. She'd been hyped, too, until

his random suggestion had blown her day out of the water.

Neither of them commented as she followed him to the lift, luckily deserted, an ascent of two floors and then along the corridor to the consultant's rooms. Lucy's lips moved silently as she repeated over and over in her head, *I am not pregnant, I am not pregnant!*

CHAPTER TWO

TEN MINUTES LATER that theory crashed and burned.

Lucy sank into the leather chair in Nikolai's office with the glass of water he'd given her in hand and tried to think.

She shook her head and closed her eyes for a moment. 'I'm my mother all over again.'

When she opened her eyes he was smiling gently. 'All mothers are their mothers.'

She sat up with a sigh. 'Well, I really am mine. On the brink of a career I've worked so hard for and I've ruined my life.' She could not believe this.

'It's been a shock. Can you remember when…?' He paused delicately and Lucy felt her cheeks warm again. This just got worse and worse. 'The night of our graduation.' Her hand crept over her stomach. This could not be happening, but the tiny bulge of her belly, something she'd been lamenting over the last week and blamed on the huge box of rocky road chocolate she'd been given, suddenly took on an ominous relevance to her queasiness.

How could she have been so stupid not to notice? She was a midwife, for pity's sake! But she'd been so excited about her job, and the house-sitting opportunity that would allow her to save money. She'd always been someone who got car sick, plane sick, excitement sick, thanks to an anxiety to please she'd thought she'd beaten.

It was a wonder she hadn't been throwing up every morning if she was pregnant, the way her stomach usually reacted to change. 'I can't be pregnant. It must be something else.'

He had such calm, sympathetic eyes. But she could tell he thought the test was valid. She guessed he had experience of this situation. Well, she didn't.

'Would you like me to run a quick ultrasound to confirm the test?'

She wanted to say, no, that would be too real. She knew a little about ultrasounds in early pregnancy. She had seen obstetricians during her practical placements using the machines on the ward when women were bleeding.

Find the sac. Foetal poles. Heartbeat if far enough along. She didn't want to know how far she had to be along. Somewhere around fourteen weeks, seeing as that had been the only time she'd ever had sex. Did she want more proof?

Maybe it was something else. Yeah, right. Fat chance. And she may as well face the reality until she decided what she was going to do and how she was going to manage this.

He was asking again, 'Would you like me to ask a nurse to come in? My receptionist has gone home. Just while we do this?'

God, no. 'No, thank you, if that's okay. Please. I don't want anyone to know.' She covered her eyes. *She* didn't want to know, but she couldn't say that.

'I understand.' His voice was low, that trace of accent

rough with sympathy, and she had the sense he really did understand a little how she was feeling.

Maybe she was even glad he was there to be a sta-biliser while she came to grips with this, except for the fact she'd have to see him almost every day at work, and he'd know her secret.

'Just do it.' Lucy climbed up onto the examination couch in his rooms, feeling ridiculous, scared and thoroughly embarrassed. Lucy closed her eyes and the mantra kept running through her head. This could not be happening.

Nikolai switched on the little portable ultrasound machine he kept in the corner of his rooms. This must have been how his sister had felt when she'd found out the worst thing a sixteen-year-old Greek Orthodox girl could find out. He just hoped there was someone here for this young woman.

He tried not to notice the unobtrusively crossed fin-gers she'd hidden down her sides as he tucked the towel across her upper abdomen to protect her purple scrubs from the gel. He didn't like her chances of the test strip being disputed by ultrasound.

He tucked another disposable sheet low in her ab-domen, definitely in professional mode, and squirted the cool jelly across the not so tiny mound of her belly. She had silky, luminous skin and he tried not to notice.

When he felt her wince under his fingers, he paused until he checked she was okay, and she nodded before he recommenced the slide of the ultrasound transducer sideways. He couldn't help but admire the control she had under the circumstances. He wondered if Chloe had been this composed.

He glanced from her to the screen and then everything else was excluded as he concentrated on the fascinating parallel universe of pelvic ultrasound.

An eerie black-and-white zone of depth and shadings. Uterus. Zoom in. Foetal spine. So the foetus was mature enough for morphology. Foetal skull. Measure circumference. Crown-rump length. Placenta. Cord. Another cord?

He blinked. 'Just shutting the blinds so I can see better.' He reached across to the wall behind her head and the remote-control curtains dulled the brightness of the Queensland sun. Zoomed in closer. Uh-oh.

The room dimmed behind Lucy's closed eyelids and then she heard it. The galloping hoofbeats of a tiny foetal heart. No other reason to have a galloping horse inside her belly except the cloppety-clop of a baby's heartbeat.

She was pregnant.

It was true. She couldn't open her eyes. Was terrified to confirm it with sight but her ears wouldn't lie.

She couldn't cope with this. Give up her hard-won career just when it was starting. Throw away the last three years of intense study, all the after-hours work to pay for it, all her dreams of being the best midwife GCG had ever seen.

Cloppety-clop, cloppety-clop. The heartbeat of her baby, growing inside her. Her child. Something shifted inside her.

She had to look. She opened her eyes just as Dr Kefes sucked in his breath and she glanced at his face. She saw the frown as he swirled the transducer around and raised his eyebrows.

What? 'Has it got two heads?' A flippant comment when she was feeling anything but flippant. Was her baby deformed? Funny how the last thing she wanted was to be pregnant but the barest hint of a problem with her tiny peanut and she was feeling…maternal?

'Sort of.' He clicked a snapshot with the machine and shifted the transducer. Clicked again.

Her stomach dropped like a stone. There was something wrong with her baby?

'What?'

'Sorry. Not what I meant.' He was looking at her with a mixture of concern and…it couldn't be wonderment surely. 'Congratulations, Lucy.'

That didn't make sense. Neither did a second heartbeat, this one slower than the other but still a clopping sound that both of them recognised. 'The measurements say you have two healthy fourteen-week foetuses.'

'I'm sorry?' He had not just said that. 'Two?'

'Twins.' He nodded to confirm his words. Held up two fingers in case she still didn't get it.

Lucy opened and shut her mouth before the words came out. 'Twins? Fourteen weeks?' Lucy squeaked, and then the world dimmed, only to return a little brighter and a whole lot louder than before—like a crash of cymbals beside her ear. She wasn't just pregnant. She was seriously, seriously pregnant.

She watched the screen zoom in and out in a haze of disbelief. Followed his finger as he pointed out legs and arms. And legs and arms. Two babies!

'I don't want twins. I don't want one,' she whispered, but even to her own ears there might be a question mark at the end of the sentence. She couldn't really be considering what she thought she was considering.

She thought briefly of Mark, her midwifery colleague already settled in Boston at his new job, a good-time guy with big plans. Their actions had been a silly impulse, regrettable but with no bad feelings, more a connection between two euphoric graduates than any kind of meeting of souls.

They'd both been sheepish after the event. The whole 'do you want coffee, can I use your bathroom', morning-after conversation that had made it very clear neither had felt the earth move—friends who should never have been lovers.

Dr Kefes broke into her thoughts and she blinked. 'If you are going to think about your options you don't have much time. In fact, you may not have any.'

Think about what? Terminating her babies that she'd heard? Seen? Was now totally aware of? She didn't know what she was going to do but she couldn't do that.

'Do they look healthy? Are they identical?' From what she'd learned about twin pregnancies there'd be more risk with identical twins than fraternal and already that was a worry.

'Looks to be one placenta but it's hard to tell. Early days, to be sure. They look fine.' His accent elongated the word *fine* and her attention zoned in on something non-traumatic—almost soothing—but he was forging on and she needed to pay attention. 'Both babies are equal size. Nothing out of the ordinary I can see.' He smiled and she was distracted for a second again from the whole tragedy. He was a serious darling, this guy. Then his words sank in.

Relief flooded over her. Her babies were fine. Relief?

She didn't know how she would manage. Certainly with no help from her own mother—how on earth would she tell her?—but she would manage. And no way was she going to blame her babies like her mother had always blamed her for ruining her life.

But that was for home. For quiet, intense thought. And she'd held this kind man up enough with her sudden drama that had blown out of all proportion into a life-changing event. Events.

She was having twins.

Holy cow.

On the first day of her new job.

She had no idea where to start with planning her life but she'd better get on with it. 'Thank you.'

Nikolai removed the transducer and nodded. As he wiped her belly he watched in awe as this slip of a girl digested her news with fierce concentration.

She was thanking him?

Well, he guessed she knew a lot more than she had half an hour ago because of him. And she seemed to be holding together pretty well. He thought of his sister again and his protective instincts kicked in. He didn't stop to think why he felt more involved than usual. But it was all a bit out of left field. 'Will you be all right?'

He wasn't sure what he'd do if she said no, and as he caught her eye, her delightful mouth curved into a smile and he saw her acknowledge that.

'Not a lot we can do if I'm not, is there?' She sat up and he helped her climb down. 'But, yes, I'll be fine. Eventually.'

He thought of his sister and the disastrous decisions she'd made in the heat of her terrifying moment all those years ago. And the ramifications now.

He thought of this woman under the care of a less-than-proficient practitioner like his sister had been, and his mind rebelled with startling force. 'I realise it's early, but if you'd like me to care for you through your pregnancy, I'd be happy to. There'd be no additional cost, of course.'

'Thank you, Dr Kefes. I think I'd like that when I

get used to the idea of being pregnant. That would be most reassuring.'

She straightened her scrubs and he gestured for her to sit in the office chair.

'Wait one moment and I'll print out a list of pathology tests I'd like you to have. The results will come to me and we'll discuss them when they come back.'

The little unexpected catches of his accent made him seem less formidable and Lucy could feel the relief that at least she wouldn't be cast adrift with the bombshell all alone.

She watched his long fingers fly across the keyboard as he opened a file on his desk computer. He made her feel safe, which was dumb because she was just a silly little girl who'd got herself pregnant, and she almost missed it when he asked for her full name, date of birth and residential address.

Luckily her mouth seemed to be working even if her brain wasn't and she managed the answers without stumbling.

He stood up. Darn, that man was tall. 'The rest we will sort out at your next visit.'

Lucy nodded, took the form, and jammed it in her bag. 'Thank you. It's been a huge day.'

'Enormous for you, of course.' Nikolai decided she still looked dazed and he resisted the urge to give her a quick hug. He would have given Chloe one but he wasn't in the habit of hugging patients or staff.

'And...' he hesitated '...may I offer you congratulations?'

'I guess congratulations are in order.' She shook her head and he didn't doubt she was only barely comprehending what her news would entail.

There was an awkward pause and he searched around

for something normal to say. 'Sister May tells me it was your first day of work. You did well and I look forward to working with you.'

He sounded patronising but had only intended to try to ease her discomfort about seeing him on the ward tomorrow.

He tried again. 'Of course your news will remain confidential until you decide to say otherwise.'

She nodded and he saw her draw a deep breath as she faced the door. She lifted her chin and he leaned in front of her to open the door. 'Allow me.'

He actually felt reassured. She would be fine. He now had some idea how strong this young woman really was. He would see that she and her babies remained as healthy as possible, he vowed as he watched her walk away.

But she did look heartbreakingly alone.

Lucy had always been alone.

Half an hour later she pushed open the door to her tiny cabana flat and the really bizarre thing was that it looked the same as when she'd left that morning.

It was she who'd changed. Drastically. And she was alone to face it. But then again when hadn't she been alone to face things? Luckily she had practice at it. The upside was that in about six months' time she'd never be alone again.

Upside? There was an upside? Where was the anxiety she should be feeling? She'd lived her whole life with that. Trying to do the right thing. She searched her feelings for anger and blame for the life-changing event that had just been confirmed, but she didn't find any.

Why aren't I angry with my babies? Didn't my mother get this feeling I'm feeling now? Almost—

no, not almost, definitely—a real connection with her babies. Maybe this was what she was meant to be. A mother.

But twins. Fourteen weeks pregnant was ridiculous. Her first pregnancy was going to be over in twenty-six weeks' time, because she'd already gone through more than a third of it.

She'd better get her head around it pretty darned quick. Let alone the known fact that twins often came earlier than expected.

She guessed she'd had her official first antenatal visit with the delicious Dr Nick.

She had to snap any of those thoughts out of her brain. Not only had he been there to see her throw up but to hear her whole sordid story of a one-night stand resulting in an unwanted pregnancy. Times two.

She frowned, and her hand crept to her tiny bulge. 'It's okay, babies, I do want you now that I know about you, but you could have waited for a more opportune time.'

Lucy rolled her eyes. 'Like in about ten years, when I'd found a man who wanted to be your father. Preferably after the wedding.' Someone like Dr Kefes?

She straightened her shoulders and patted her belly. 'But don't worry. I'll give you all the love I never had and there will be no string of uncles staying over. If I don't meet a one hundred per cent perfect daddy for you, we'll do this ourselves.'

Her voice died away and she glanced around the empty room. She was going mad already. She'd bet Dr Kefes thought she was mad.

Twenty-two, single and taking on twins instead of the career she'd worked so hard to achieve.

She had almost been able to feel his soothing persona. He'd been very kind. Incredibly supportive considering he didn't know her. She could understand why women fell a little in love with their obstetricians if they were all like him.

Though she didn't think there could be a lot of tall, dark and dreamy docs out there with such a delicious hint of a foreign accent.

But at the end of everything, she would be the one holding the babies, and she'd better stop thinking that some demi-god was going to swoop in and lend her a hand.

This was her responsibility and hers alone.

She glanced at the tiny cabana she'd been lucky enough to score in exchange for house-sitting the mansion out front, and she was thankful. *Be thankful.* She needed to remember that. If the owners decided to sell, something else would turn up. She had to believe that.

And she would find a way to support her babies. She'd just have to save every penny she could until she finished work.

At least she'd get maternity leave—or would she if she was fourteen weeks pregnant on her first day? More things to find out.

But they did have a crèche at the hospital so eventually she'd be able to go back. If Flora May would have her after she told her the news. She put her head in her hands.

And how would she tell her mother?

A kilometre away, Nikolai threw his keys on the hall table inside the door of his flat and pulled off his tie. What a day. And not just with work.

He wasn't sure why he was so rattled by his encounter with Lucy the midwife, and her news, but he guessed it had to do with the day starting with his sister's phone call. He'd obviously associated the two women in his mind.

That explained his bizarre feeling of connection with young Lucy. And that was what she was. Young. Barely over twenty, and he was a good ten years older so it had to be an avuncular or older-brother protectiveness. He'd just have to watch it in case she got any ideas.

Because he certainly didn't have any.

Maybe it hadn't been so clever to offer to look after her during her pregnancy, but it had seemed right at the time. And he genuinely wanted her to have the best care.

But when the next day at work he only saw Lucy in the distance, she waved once discreetly because both of them were busy with their own workload, and by the end of the day his concerns had seemed foolish.

He wasn't piqued she hadn't made any effort to speak to him. Of course not. His concerns were ridiculous. But it seemed he had no worries that she might take liberties with his offer.

Then the day suddenly got busier and Lucy and her problems disappeared into the back of his mind.

The busyness of the ward continued for almost a fortnight, so much so that the staff were counting back in the calendars to see what had happened around this time ten months ago. Solar eclipse? Power blackout?

There was an unofficial competition to see who could come up with the most likely reason for the surge in births.

It was Lucy's fifth shift in a row and she was finding it harder to get out of bed at six in the morning.

'Come on, lazybones,' she grumbled to herself as she sat up on the side of the bed. 'You've got no stamina. You think it's going to be easier when you've got to get two little bodkins organised every three hours for feeds?'

She stood up and rubbed her back. 'They all say it's going to get quieter at work again soon. You can do this.' And she still hadn't told her mother. She'd told Mark and he'd offered money. And no strings. That was a good thing because she knew in her heart an unwilling Mark wasn't the answer for either of them. The last thing she wanted was her babies to see her in an unhappy relationship.

When Nikolai saw Lucy he could tell she was starting to feel the frenetic pace. Her usual determined little walk had slowed and he didn't notice her smile as often.

The next time he saw her he decided she looked far too pale and he couldn't remember any results from the blood tests he'd ordered a fortnight ago.

He added 'Follow up with Lucy' to his list of tasks for the day and tracked her down towards the end of the shift.

'One moment, Lucy.'

She stopped and smiled tiredly up at him. 'Yes, Doctor?'

He felt like offering her a chair. Wasn't anyone looking after this girl? It had been hard enough for him to look after Chloe and he'd been the same age as Lucy was now. And a man, not a slip of a girl.

It was tough making ends meet when you were trying to get through uni and feed yourself. He wondered if she was eating properly before he realised she was waiting for him to finish his sentence.

'Sorry.' He glanced around but no one was near them. 'I wondered why I haven't seen those results yet.'

Lucy racked her brain. An hour of the shift to go and

she was finding it hard not to yawn. Now he wanted results and she had no idea whose he was talking about. For which patient? She frowned. 'Was I supposed to give you some results?'

'Yours. Antenatal screening.' He looked so hard at her she felt like he'd put her under the microscope.

'You look pale.'

She felt pale, if that was possible. She'd forgotten the tests. She ran back over that momentous day, back to his rooms. Yes, he'd given her forms, and the form was still scrunched in the bottom of her bag. Maybe there was something Freudian about that.

She sighed. 'I keep meaning to get them done. Maybe I'm not ready to tell the world.'

She saw him glance at her stomach and raise his eyebrows. She looked down, too. And didn't think it showed much yet.

He was frowning and he rarely frowned. That was one of the things she liked about this guy. One of the many things.

'I'd like you to do them today, if you could, please. Outside the hospital if you want to. But if you have them done internally there will be no charge for the pathology.'

And pathology tests could be expensive. Expenses she needed to cut back on. 'Big incentive.' She nodded. Just so he knew she meant it. 'I'll go after work.'

He stayed where he was. Looking so calm and collected and immaculate. She felt like a dishrag. Her back hurt. What else did he want?

'And could you make an appointment to come and see me in two days? I'll let my secretary know.'

Lucy laughed for the first time that day. It actually felt good. She could even feel the tension drop from her shoulders and reminded herself she needed to shed a few chuckles more often. She didn't want to forget that. Her mother had rarely laughed while she had been growing up.

But two days? It seemed she wasn't the only one who was tired. 'Two days is a Sunday. I don't think your secretary will be take an appointment on that one. But I will make it for Monday.'

Nick smiled back at her and she felt her cheeks warm. She frowned at herself and him. He shouldn't smile at emotional, hormonal women like that. Especially ones who were planning to be single mothers of twins.

She was never going to feel second best again and he made her feel like she wanted to be better than she was. The guy was just too perfect. For her anyway.

'Thanks for the reminder. Have to go.' She turned and walked back to the desk and she could hear his footsteps walking away. She could imagine the sight. The long strides. The commanding tilt of his head. Not fair.

'You okay there, Palmer?' Flora May was staring at her under her grizzled brows. She glanced at the receding back of Dr Kefes. 'Is he giving you a hard time?'

'No. Of course not. He's been very kind.' Though she smiled at her fierce protector. 'I'm just tired.' Flora May did not look convinced. Lucy tried again. 'Not sure if I'm not coming down with something.'

Flora and Lucy were very similar in the way they viewed their vocation, and Lucy appreciated having Flora on her side. Never warm and fuzzy, Flora's no-nonsense advice was always valid, and usually made Lucy smile.

'You do look peaky. Pale and limp probably describes you.'

Lucy had to smile at the unflattering description. 'Thank you, Sister.'

'If you're unwell, go to the staff clinic at Emergency. Nobody else wants to catch anything. Either way, you can leave early. I'll do your handover. You get here fifteen minutes early every day and you're the last to leave. You've earned some time in lieu.'

The idea was very attractive.

Flora's lips twitched. 'But don't expect it every week.'

'I certainly won't.' Lucy looked at her mentor. Maybe now was a good time. She'd hate Flora to find out from someone else or, worse, through a rumour. 'Can I see you for a moment, Sister? In private.'

'Of course.' Flora gestured to her office.

Lucy drew a deep breath and Flora frowned at her obvious trepidation. 'Spit it out, Palmer.'

'I'm pregnant.' Lucy searched Flora's face for extreme disappointment. Anger. Disgust. She'd suspected Flora had plans for her training and knew she had been instrumental in choosing Lucy over other applicants. But Flora's expression didn't change. Except to soften.

She stepped forward and put her arm around Lucy's shoulders and gave her a brief, awkward hug before she snapped back into her professional self.

'That explains a lot,' she said gruffly. Cleared her throat. 'You've been a little more preoccupied than I expected.' To Lucy's stunned relief she even smiled. 'When, in fact, you've been a lot more focused than you could be expected to be.' Flora gazed past Lucy's shoulder while she thought about it.

Then she concentrated on Lucy again. 'And Dr Kefes is looking after you? He knows?'

Lucy blinked and nodded. How did Flora know this

stuff? 'I forgot to have some tests and he was reminding me.'

'He's a good man.' Then she said something strange. 'Don't go falling for him. Easy people to fall for, obstetricians.'

Didn't she know it! A mental picture of Dr Kefes, five minutes ago, smiling down at her and her own visceral response highlighted that dilemma. No way was she going down that demoralising path. 'I won't. I'm not that stupid.'

Flora sniffed. Her piercing gaze stayed glued on Lucy's face. 'Is there a man on the scene? Some help coming?'

Lucy shook her head. She wasn't anxious to go into it but, judging by the sigh, it seemed Flora had expected that. 'Your family?'

Lucy shook her head again. She could dream her mother would turn into a supportive, caring, helpful shoulder to lean on but it was highly unlikely. She so dreaded that conversation but after surviving telling Flora today, maybe she could even hope a little that it would be as bad as she dreaded.

'I've got your back, Palmer. Go home now. Rest. You still look peaky. And if you want help or advice—ask!'

Lucy nodded past the lump in her throat. How had she been so lucky to end up with Flora as a boss?

Flora smiled at her. 'Look after yourself, Palmer. I still have big plans for you.'

Now she felt like crying, and if she didn't get out of here quickly she'd disgrace herself by throwing her sobbing self onto the starched front of her boss.

Lucy almost ran from the ward, past Cass who was on day shifts for a few weeks, and in her hasty departure she didn't see the speculative look that followed her.

She also forgot all about the blood tests she was supposed to get as she pressed the button for the lift and escape.

The doors opened. When she stepped in Nikolai was standing at the back of the lift like her nemesis. 'Are you going to Pathology now?'

Lucy blinked. She felt like smacking her forehead but instead refused to be goaded into saying she'd forgotten again. 'Are you following me?'

Thick, dark, eyebrows lifted. 'I imagine that would be difficult from the inside of a lift. Not being able to see through the walls.'

She played the words back in her head and winced. Impolite and ungrateful. It wasn't Dr Kefes's fault she felt physically and emotionally exhausted. 'Sorry. And, yes.' She sighed. 'I'll go to Pathology now.'

The lift stopped on another floor and two intense, white-coated doctors entered, and the conversation died a natural death.

Lucy recognised one of the newcomers, Callie Richards, the paediatrician who was looking after Sally's baby. They both nodded at Nick but the tension between them was palpable to the other two in the lift and, fancifully, Lucy decided the air was actually shimmering.

It seemed other people had dramas, too. The man raised his eyebrows at Nick, who didn't change his expression, and Callie offered a forced smile to Lucy, who smiled back awkwardly.

One floor down the late arrivals stepped out and as the doors shut Lucy let out the breath she hadn't realised she'd been holding in a little whistle. She looked at Nikolai. 'Who's the guy?'

Nick smiled. 'Cade Coleman, prenatal surgeon from Boston. And you've met Callie Richards, the neonatal specialist. She's in charge of the NICU here and is looking after Sally's baby.'

'Yep. I remember her. She seems nice. It was just him I didn't know. I guess I'll recognise everyone soon.'

They reached the ground floor and the lift light changed to indicate 'up'. Lucy realised she hadn't directed the lift to take her further down to the laboratory.

Nikolai shook his head and pressed the lower-ground button for Pathology to override the person above. He put his hand across the doors to hold them open. 'Are you working on Monday?'

'One in the afternoon.'

'Perhaps you'd like to see me to get your results before you start. My rooms. Twelve-thirty? In case you forget to make the appointment.'

Ooh. It was her turn to give him the look. 'Fine. Thank you.' As he took his arm away from the doors she said, 'Are you this helpful to all your pregnant ladies?'

He shrugged and she couldn't read the expression on his face. 'Only the really vague ones who forget to have their bloods done.'

'Touché,' she said cheekily, and he smiled. She watched him walk away until the doors shut and the lift sailed downwards. Well, she had been vague to forget again but she needed to sleep. As soon as she got home she was going to bed and sleeping the clock round.

Nick's hand tightened on his briefcase as he strode to the doctors' car park. She had a point. But the memories of Chloe, gaunt and drawn, haunted him and when he'd seen Lucy was looking so tired it had brought it all back. He needed to stop worrying about her. She wasn't Chloe, neither was she his responsibility. Although even

Chloe would have a fit if she thought he still felt the need to keep her under his wing.

His phone rang. His registrar. Thoughts of Lucy shifted to the back of his mind again as he turned back to the hospital.

CHAPTER THREE

THAT NIGHT, AFTER a nap and crossing her fingers after her less-than-traumatic disclosure to Flora May, Lucy decided to talk to her mother. She glanced at the clock. It was too early for the dinner date her mother always had before clubbing with her friends on Friday nights but hopefully late enough to be after the ritual bath and nail preparation that took place prior to departure.

'Mum? It's Lucy.' There was a vague affirmative and Lucy bit back a sigh. One day she was going to stop hoping for a shriek of pleasure from her mother that she'd rung.

'I know you're going out. Can I talk for a minute?'

The conversation went downhill from there. If being told she had always known she would let her mother down, done the exact thing her mother had told her not to do, been called an immoral, stupid little girl, being told that no way was she ever minding her brats or even admitting to being a grandmother counted as a conversation going downhill.

Lucy was pretty sure it was, because she could feel herself curling into a protective ball as the tirade continued. She just got more numb and wasn't even aware of the tears as they rolled down her cheeks.

When her mother paused for breath, Lucy finished

by whispering, 'And by the way, I'm having twins.'
There was a further stunned silence and Lucy decided
to put the phone down gently. Enough.

Yep. It had been as bad as she'd feared. Probably
worse. She sucked in a breath and forced her shoulders
to loosen from the deathlike squeeze she had them in.

Her hand crept to her belly. She wasn't having brats.
She was having gorgeous babies and maybe they would
be better off without a vitriolic grandmother. Maybe she
would finally be able to separate her mother's idea of
who she was from her own version. It might take a bit
of practice but she had six months to do it before her
babies were born.

Surprisingly, or perhaps not surprisingly given her
exhaustion and mental distress, Lucy slept most of the
night for the first time in ages.

On Saturday she did the bare minimum of housework
and lazed and snoozed all day, recharging her batteries
for next week's onslaught.

She started a journal, wrote down her thoughts and
all the things she had to be grateful for, and began to
talk to her babies. It was amazing what a difference a
small change like that made.

By Sunday morning she was rested and felt more like
her old self. In fact, she felt better than better. Maybe
it was knowing that the dreaded call, despite being as
horrific as she'd dreaded, was over. Done.

Some time in the night she'd felt the first real joy
of what was to come. So this was her path. What she
couldn't change, she would just do better.

Her midwifery would be put on hold, but at least it
might have prepared her a bit for what was ahead.

Pregnancy, birth, maybe not twins but, hey, twice

the joy. She'd been chosen for that double blessing for a reason, she just hadn't figured out what that reason was.

So, it was a beautiful day, her stomach growled with hunger for the first time in weeks, and she lived in a fabulous part of the world with the ocean right outside her landlord's front door. What wasn't to celebrate?

Filled with new vigour, Lucy tidied her cabana and afterwards scooted around the big house, plucked dead leaves off ornamental ferns, cleaned the aquarium filter and steam-mopped the outside terrace because the salt was crusty underfoot from the storm a few days ago.

Besides, she loved the front terrace, where she could look out over the white sand just behind the boundary fence, watch the paddle-boarders and hope to catch a glimpse of a whale or a dolphin.

As she hummed a country ballad the gate screeched as she took the garbage out, so she hunted out the lubricant spray, sang a few words and patted her stomach as she wandered back to fix it. 'We'll be okay, kiddos.'

Nick's Sunday morning wasn't going as planned. He'd knocked on Chloe's door to see if she was interested in them having breakfast together. It was handy having a sister in the flat next to his. He was starving and maybe they could catch up.

But after the third knock nobody came to the door, so she was either out or not answering. He'd go for a jog and see if she was there when he came back. He tried to check the impulse to find out where she was or who she was with. Just check she was okay, he reminded himself.

Nick was sick of his own company—which was almost unheard of—and just a little bored. As he set off he reminded himself that exercise often worked to shut the voices down.

The beach felt great under the soles of his runners but while the long jog along the sand had helped his restlessness it had also stoked up his appetite for that iconic Sunday breakfast—one of his favourite times on the Gold Coast. With so many great places showing off the ocean, choice was a problem but the idea of eating alone, again, was less than appealing.

Not that there wasn't activity and people everywhere. Kids were learning to be lifesavers on the beach with their little tied-on caps and colourful swimmers. Paddle-boarders skimmed the backs of waves and made him wish he'd bought one. Apparently it was a useful and not sexually orientated exercise diversion—as his sister had wryly commented.

He didn't know why Chloe had a thing about his carefree love life. He wasn't promiscuous, he just didn't feel the need to belong to anybody.

He was happy to concentrate on his work and have fun with like-minded women. He wasn't out to break anybody's heart, and relationships were for dalliance, not drama.

Still, a diversion would be nice, he thought as his shoes slapped the footpath and he finally spied a shapely little surfer girl in a tiny bright skirt and floaty top ahead, kneeling beside the driveway of one of the mansions. She was doing something to a gate. He couldn't help his appreciative smile as he jogged closer.

The sunlight danced in a deep auburn cascade of hair that hid her face and the way she was leaning over promised the sort of shapely curves men liked and women didn't.

So it was a shock when she looked up to see hazel

eyes and a rosebud mouth he already knew. Not a babe. It was Lucy. Pregnant-with-twins Lucy.

His social skills dropped with his confusion. 'Hey, stranger.'

She grinned at him. Looked him up and down and shook her head. 'Ha. I'm not the strange one. I'm not wearing shorts and joggers with black socks.'

'Ouch.' He looked down at his trunks and runners, and decided to throw away the socks, even though they barely showed above his shoes. He'd thought he looked okay. 'I'll have you know this is the latest in trendy jog wear.'

'My bad, then.' She didn't look sorry. She sat back and wiped her hair out of her eyes and the thick mane flashed like fire in the sunlight. Funny he hadn't noticed her hair that much at work. 'So, where do trendy joggers run to?'

He blinked. 'Mostly to and from the beach. And back to the hospital apartment building where a lot of the trendy staff stay.' He sounded like an idiot, so he glanced away and pointed to a tall building a block back from the ocean.

'Wondered where that was.'

He looked back at her and the slight breeze rippled her hair as she turned her head to look. He'd never had a thing for redheads before—but now he could see the attraction. He'd heard they had a tendency for fire and passion and he could just imagine young Lucy letting fly. The thought made him smile even more.

'I didn't know it was so close to the hospital,' she said. 'Been there long?'

His mind was five per cent on the conversation and ninety-five on admiring the view. 'Not that long. I live next door to my sister, Chloe. Two years now. Very convenient.'

'Someone said you had a sister who was a nurse at the hospital.' She nodded, and everything on the top half of her body wobbled a bit. He tried not to stare at her cleavage.

Things were getting foggy. 'Bless the grapevine. Yep.' Why was he brain dead? 'We used to share but she wanted her own place and couldn't see any reason to shift.' He was rambling. 'It's close enough to the hospital that I can walk if I want to. Or run in an emergency. Most times I drive because usually I'm going somewhere later.'

She nodded again and this time he made sure he didn't look south.

His mouth was dry. From the jogging, of course. He could seriously do with a drink. 'Is this your house?' He couldn't keep the surprise out of his voice but when she laughed he acknowledged relief. The last thing he wanted to do was offend her. She was having things tough enough.

Her lips curved. 'Yeah, right. I'm a closet millionaire.'

She raised her eyebrows haughtily and grinned. 'I'm the house-sitter. These people are friends of an older couple who used to put up with me visiting a lot when I was a kid. They were the first people I told about the babies. Nearly time to go public.'

He thought about that. About the hospital and the rumours, and he consoled himself it would blow over in a week. He'd try to make sure he checked she was okay when it all blew up. 'Seems a very nice place to stay. You living in the house?'

'No.' When she shook her head it was better than nodding because everything really jiggled.

He should go but he enjoyed the way she talked. Bubbly and relaxed. Not like the women he usually hung out with, who were always on their best behaviour. He knew that Lucy wasn't trying to attract him. Which was a good thing because she needed a fling like she needed a hole in the head. And he didn't do relationships, and you couldn't have much else with a woman who was pregnant by someone else.

'I have the cabana out back, which suits me fine. I just open the house up every couple of days, let the breeze blow through, water the indoor plants. Feed the fish. That kind of stuff.'

She was sort of restful, too. He could picture her pottering around. Maybe humming off key. 'Spray the rusty gate kinda stuff?'

She waved the can. 'That's me. Handy Lucy.'

'Nice.' He refused to think about where he wanted to put his hands. Instead, he said, 'Would you like to go for breakfast?'

Where the heck had that come from? Nick couldn't believe he'd just said that. Hell, and he'd told himself he was going to be careful to keep it professional.

But apparently that thought couldn't stop him from embellishing the offer. 'Maybe bacon and eggs down at the surf club near Elephant Rock? My shout. We could try and get a table on the veranda and soak in some Vitamin D.'

He didn't even recognise what he was saying. Some devil inside was using his mouth. Didn't it know she was going to be a patient of his as well as a work colleague? This was an invitation with disaster written all over it.

Lucy's face lit up with the happiest smile he'd seen all week. Too late to back out, then. So maybe having a devil using his mouth was worth it if she got that much of a kick out of company.

Her chin jutted as if she expected an argument. 'I'll pay my own way, thanks, but I love that place.'

Independent, then. He'd already guessed that. But he'd bet she was lonely, too.

'And I understand sunlight is very important for pregnant women.' She grinned. 'Gee. Breakfast on the beach and my appetite's back.'

A glow expanded in his chest, because he could have a cooked breakfast and not have to eat it alone, and he'd made a girl happy. Three good things from one action. 'I'll grab my car and meet you back here, in…' he glanced at his watch '…say, fifteen minutes?'

'Perfect.'

Nick lifted one hand as he jogged off towards the tall building Lucy could see further up the road. She recognised the bulk of the hospital behind and how it could be useful to have the consultants' units so close.

So it seemed Dr Kefes jogged by her door regularly. This morning she'd had her headphones in and hadn't heard him approach so it had been a shock when he'd stopped. She'd thought him just a well-built jogger and had been happy to admire the fitness machine, until she'd recognised him, then she'd been bowled over by the sheer physical presence of him.

That must have been where the black-sock comment had come from. She'd felt like smacking her forehead when that had popped out.

'Just trying to make him human,' she muttered, and bit back a giggle. She should be aghast at herself for teasing him—but she wasn't, and he hadn't seemed to mind. He probably had women sucking up to him everywhere. She'd never been a toady—except to her

mother, but she was going to train herself out of that—
and wasn't going to start now.

Lucy gave the gate a final generous spray of lubricant and stood up.

And she darned well refused to feel nervous about
going for breakfast with him. Dr Kefes. Nikolai. He
hadn't actually said she could call him Nick but she'd
worry about that later. She hadn't felt this good for
weeks so she may as well enjoy it, and now there was
a bit of unexpected excitement in her day.

Who knew when the next pregnancy ailment would
strike? And she was in for double dose when it did
come.

As for having breakfast with a consultant at her
work who'd also offered to be her obstetrician, well,
she wasn't going to get out of line, and there was no way
he would. No reason they couldn't be friends.

By the time Nick arrived to pick her up Lucy was
standing at the gate in a yellow sundress, complete, he
couldn't help noticing, with bra. He saw the straps and
stifled his disappointment. Stop it.

He leaned across and opened the passenger door for
her because he could see she wasn't going to wait for
him to get out and do the job properly.

She slid in, accompanied by a drift of some light and
spicy perfume that smelt like the spring flowers Chloe
kept around her flat, and she must have felt comfortable because she slid her sandals off.

Suddenly his car took on a new life. There was
something earthy and incredibly sexy about bare brown
toes rubbing over each other as she settled back in the
leather seat.

She sighed blissfully and his day got better. 'Always
fancied a convertible.'

He laughed. She made him laugh. 'Me, too.'

'This car would go with my house.'

He nodded sagely. 'Hell with a stroller, though.'

'Especially a twin stroller.' Their eyes met and he was pleased and surprised to see the serenity in hers. He admired her more each time they talked.

He'd have to watch that. 'I see you're at peace with your decision.'

'Yes. Thank you, Dr Kefes.'

'Nick.' He pulled over into a parking space right outside the restaurant that someone had just pulled out from, parallel to the beach. 'You must be very lucky to have around. I usually park twenty minutes away from this place.'

Her head was back against the headrest and her eyes were shut as the sun bathed her in bright yellow light. 'Lucky Lucy. That's me.'

He soaked the sight in for a few seconds, shook his head at her ability to just enjoy the moment and then leaned forward and removed his keys from the ignition. 'Handy and lucky? Worth cultivating.'

She opened her eyes. 'Hopefully someone will think so one day.' There was no self-pity in the statement. Just truth. 'I'm starving.'

He laughed again. 'So am I.' Typically, she was out of the car before he could get to her door.

They scored a table right on the corner of the big verandah overlooking the beach. 'More luck,' Nick murmured, and Lucy just smiled.

The salt-laden breeze blew their big umbrella backwards and forwards a little so that most of the time they were in the shade but every few seconds a brief wash of sunlight dusted her shoulders with golden light. Nick decided the view was great in every direction.

'So, have you thought about what you'll do when the babies are born?'

She rested her cute chin on her fingers. She made him feel so relaxed. 'My next-door neighbour used to say, "Planning to make a plan is not a plan", so, yes. I have a plan.'

He was intrigued. 'And that is?'

She straightened. 'I'll work as long as I can then hopefully I'll get maternity leave from work. It won't be paid but from what Flora May said I think I get to keep my job. The hospital has a crèche, so I'll go back to work one day a week part-time as soon as possible, and that's only eight hours away from them. That's not unreasonable.'

She shrugged. 'When we all get used to that I'll do two days and so on. Not quite sure how I'll survive financially with that but that's a few months ahead. And I've saved a little money.' She grinned at him. 'Luckily, I'm not a material girl.'

It sounded pretty shaky for a plan but she hadn't had much time. 'What about your parents?'

Her face changed and he wondered if she really was shrinking into the chair or if he was just imagining it. She looked away out over the waves and he seriously regretted having asked the question, judging by her response.

'Parent.' She shrugged and still didn't meet his eyes. 'Only ever had Mum, though she's a two-edged sword. She always said I ruined her life.'

'Your mother?' He tried to imagine an older Lucy with a nasty mouth.

She shrugged and he decided she had the best shoulders in the restaurant.

'Imagine one of those anxious-to-please, quiet little

girls who could never get anything right?' She forced a smile and Nick decided it actually hurt to watch. Maybe she wasn't so together after all.

He couldn't quite put this girl together with the one who had dragged him in to see her patient on her first day.

'Anyway. That little girl was me. The only time I ever felt like a winner was when I accepted my midwifery degree. And Mum didn't make it to see that.'

But, still, her mother? Nick thought. 'So she won't help you?'

'Mum?' Lucy laughed but it wasn't the sound he'd heard before. Surprisingly there was no bitterness in the sound, just the scrape of raw nerves. 'She taught me to rely on myself. That's a pretty helpful trait.'

He guessed his own parents had done that to Chloe and him as well. 'And you're not bitter?' He certainly was. Not for himself now but for the young teen his sister had been when they'd cast her off, and him for supporting her.

He guessed his parents had hurt him the way he could see Lucy's mother had hurt her, but he hadn't really had time to worry about it. He'd been more worried about getting food on the table and pushing Chloe to study.

Lucy was staring over the waves and fancifully he wondered why the sun wasn't playing with her any more.

'Mum managed as well as she could with her own disappointments. Now she is a material girl.'

She straightened and he saw a little more of the midwife advocate he'd seen on the ward. 'If there's one thing I know, it's that my children won't feel a burden. I'm ambitious for my midwifery, but I'll be there for them no matter what.' It seemed she could fight for others but not for herself. He'd think about that later.

'My mother told me she'd left it too late to get rid of me, and I'm so pleased I can say I made the choice to keep my children.'

Hell. Her mother had told her that? Nick had thought his parents were insensitive but he couldn't imagine what being told that would do to the psyche of a young woman.

But she'd moved on. At least in this conversation. 'I'd hoped that by the time I had kids my husband would have a warm and fuzzy mother who would tuck me under her wing and do girl things with me. Looks like that's not going to happen.'

He didn't usually mention it, in fact, he couldn't re-member ever mentioning it, but maybe it would help if she knew other people had failures as parents. 'Or you could end up with a mother like ours who just wiped Chloe and me out of her life and broke off all contact.'

'What do you mean?'

They'd behaved as though their two children hadn't existed. My word, he remembered that, the way he'd pleaded with them to soften towards his sixteen-year-old sister, when all he'd wanted to do had been to tear strips off them for their unforgiveable behaviour.

He'd taken too many bitter rebuffs for Chloe to ever forgive them.

It had been a defining moment in his life to learn that people could choose to exclude others regardless of how much pain they'd caused. It was also the perfect reason not to become emotionally involved, and that mantra had worked for him very well.

And Chloe was suffering because she still couldn't

do the same. 'Refused to communicate. Didn't answer calls when I tried to get them to talk to Chloe.'

'That sucks. I'm sorry.' Then she looked away and he almost missed her further words. 'But you have your sister. I had no one.'

She lifted her chin. 'Sorry. I'm spoiling your breakfast with my complaining. I didn't mean to. And I'll have my babies soon.' She lifted her chin higher. 'I'm tough. I'll give up whatever I need to for my babies to have a good life and I will always be there for them. Money and possessions aren't important. Love is.'

This had got pretty deep pretty fast, but he'd asked for it. He shifted in his seat. Contrarily, now he wanted out of this discussion. He tried for a lighter note. 'Money buys you sports cars.'

She raised those haughty brows. 'Yeah, but you can't fit twin strollers in them.'

The waitress arrived to take their orders, the conversation bounced back to impersonal, and thankfully the sun came back and danced on her. He didn't know if he'd directed it that way or if she had, but seagulls wheeled overhead, and the breeze made him want to push the hair out of Lucy's eyes.

They talked about the hospital, the great facilities the birth suites had, their young mum's baby's progress and how the young mum had been so diligent in the special care nursery after her own discharge. They were both careful not to mention anyone's names, and it made it more intimate that only the two of them knew who they were talking about.

To his disappointment, the meals were on the table in no time.

For the first time he wished the usually 'snowed under with orders' staff were not so efficient because by the way Lucy was tucking into her meal they'd be out of there in half an hour.

They ate silently until Lucy sat back with an embarrassed smile. 'Wow. I even beat you.'

He admired her empty plate. 'I can see you were hungry.'

She shrugged. 'Rather feed me for a week than a fortnight, eh? But up until today I haven't been eating well.'

She was too cute. 'I think you're cured.'

She patted her round stomach. 'Not too cured, I hope. I don't want to look like a balloon by the time these babies are born.'

His eyes slid over her appreciatively. 'I don't think you have to worry. But I'll mention to your obstetrician to keep an eye on your weight.'

She wagged a finger at him. 'You do that.' Then she began to fiddle with her teaspoon and he wondered what was coming. You never knew with this woman. 'I need to thank you.'

He shifted uncomfortably. 'What for.'

Hazel eyes caught his. 'For looking after me on the day the bomb dropped.'

He glanced at the children playing in the surf. 'My pleasure.'

She laughed and he looked back at her. Couldn't avoid the urge at the sound. 'I'm sure it wasn't. I fell to pieces.'

Her eyes crinkled and her white teeth were just a little crooked. That tiny unevenness made her seem more real than other women he'd dated. Seriously delightful. 'I didn't see any pieces. I though you held up remarkably well.'

She threw back her head and laughed and he saw a

man at another table look their way with an appreciative smile. Nick stared and the guy looked away.

Lucy was oblivious to anyone else. 'Come on. I threw up in front of you.'

That made him smile. 'But very tidily.'

He shrugged. 'I didn't actually see anything...' He shook his head mournfully. 'And have tried not to think about it.'

She laughed again and he enjoyed that he'd made it happen this time. 'I had no idea you were mad.'

'I hide it.' He shrugged.

She pretended to clap her hands. 'Very well, if I may say so. Anyway. Thank you. If it wasn't for you I would have been alone.'

She shouldn't have been. It made him wonder just where this one-night stand was now. It took two to tango. 'What about the father?'

She brushed the unknown man away and, contrarily, now Nick winced in sympathy for the mystery sperm donor. 'I don't expect anything more from him. My mother managed when my own father walked out.'

'But does he know?' Nick still had issues with that. He'd certainly want to know if a woman he'd helped make a baby with hadn't told him.

Almost as if she'd read his thoughts, she said, 'I've told him. He had a right to that information. He suggested termination.'

'Did that offend you?' He'd sort of put it out there, too, not that he was an advocate, especially after Chloe's disaster. Did she hold that against him?

'It clarified his level of commitment. Although he sent a generous amount of money for a termination and said to use it as emergency fund if I didn't use it for that. I won't be putting him on the birth certificate, or expect financial assistance again, unless the babies want that sometime in the future.'

Some conversation that must have been. 'Is that wise?' She was so clinical. 'Won't you need more financial help?' Judging by her 'plan', he thought she might.

'He's a friend. You don't ask friends for money. Even ones you accidentally sleep with. He has his own life and these are my children.'

In this sense she was so tough. So focused. And if he admitted it, just a little scary in the way she seemed to have taken this momentous news in her stride.

It was in his culture to expect women to need help. Greek heritage was all about family. Except for his own toxic parents.

Chloe had allowed him to be there when she'd needed him, but she was his sister. And she was less amenable now. This woman was nothing to him and he was nothing to her. He should be glad she could stand on her own feet.

Lucy heard the brave words leave her mouth and almost believed them. She pushed away the tiny ache for someone else to share some of the responsibility at least. It certainly wasn't this lovely doctor's problem. A shame, that.

She needed to man up. The thought made her smile. Like one of those insects that changed sex once they were pregnant, except she was going the other way. Actually, quite a disquieting thought. 'Thank you for bringing me with you for breakfast.'

Ouch, Lucy thought, she sounded like a little girl after a party. But he was too sweet. Too darned handsome and masculine and eminently capable of carrying responsibility. She rummaged in her purse and brought

out the correct change for her meal and slipped it discreetly under her napkin.

Thankfully he didn't say anything. Just picked it up
and put it in his pocket. 'I gather you're ready to go?'

'Yes, please.' She picked up her bag and stood before
he could come round to her chair. She had the idea she
was frustrating his attempts to treat her like a lady but
she wasn't his date and she wanted to make that clear.

Judging by his face, he got it. 'I'll fix this up and
meet you outside, then.'

Good. She'd have time to go to the ladies' room. She
smiled to herself. Being pregnant certainly affected her
bladder capacity.

Nick tried not to watch her scurry off and he remembered she was pregnant. How could he have forgotten
that? There was no reason they couldn't be friends but
the sooner he dropped her home the better. Afterwards
he might go and buy himself a paddleboard and take
some of that frustration out on the waves.

CHAPTER FOUR

BEFORE LUNCH ON Monday Nick had a strange conversation with Callie Richards, ostensibly a neonatologist discussing a case with attending obstetrician.

Nick wasn't sure how Sally's baby in NICU had somehow ended up with Cade Coleman, the prenatal surgeon, who was apparently giving Callie a hard time. Which was a bit of a joke because Callie loved to straight-talk, too, and the whole hospital was buzzing with the sparks those two were striking off each other.

Callie was a good friend, but there was no chemistry between them, despite their pretty similar outlooks on relationships and no-strings sex.

He thought to himself with amusement, as Callie raved, that any chance of that was out there amongst the waves, with Cade now on the scene.

He put up his hand to stem the flow. 'You fancy him.'

Callie stopped. Shocked. 'I do not.'

Nick raised his eyebrows. 'So this is you being oblivious is it?'

She glared at him. 'I'm just sick of being growled at.'

'I've seen him work in prenatal surgery.' Nick shrugged. 'The guy's intense, he cares, and he's even great with the parents. He's allowed a little growling.'

'I'm whining, aren't I?' Callie drooped.

'A little.' Nick couldn't help but smile.

Callie lifted her head and drew in an audible breath. 'I needed that.' She picked up her briefcase. 'You're right. Thanks.' And she sailed out.

Nick shook his head and glanced at his watch.

Lucy should be here in a minute. He'd given her the time slot he usually reserved for completing the paperwork from the morning and he guessed he could start it now.

He sat down at the desk and tried to concentrate to stop himself opening the door to see if she'd arrived yet. Obviously she hadn't because his secretary would have rung. He picked up his pen again and his eyes strayed to his watch.

Lucy turned up for her first real antenatal appointment at the hospital and despite the fact she was going straight to work from there, she'd tried to be inconspicuous by dressing in loose civilian clothes.

It didn't work. The first person she saw as she opened Nick's office door was the Callie Richards, who was just leaving.

'Hello, there, Lucy isn't it? You're the midwife who looked after Sally, aren't you?'

'Yes, how is little Zac?' Lucy could feel the heat in her cheeks as she smiled and nodded, pretending it was wonderful that the senior paediatrician had recognised her entering an obstetrician's office. On one level it was, but on the other, not so great.

Callie must have picked up her discomfort because her expression changed. 'Great.' And then, cryptically, she said, 'No problem, by the way.' She smiled reassuringly. 'Have a good day.'

This was silly, feeling embarrassed. It was all going to come out pretty soon anyway. 'You, too.'

Callie left and as Lucy crossed to the reception desk, her cheeks only got pinker. This was terrible.

Nick opened his door. 'Lucy?'

The receptionist looked up and waved her through and as she walked past him into his rooms she started to feel better.

Nick seemed so broad and tall and she realised she really liked that about him. It was reassuring for some reason. He was a man to have beside you in a dark alley. Or a single-parent pregnancy.

At five feet seven she wasn't short, but he made her feel tiny as he shut the door behind her. She crossed the room, sat in the seat she remembered from nearly three weeks ago and tried to relax.

So much had changed in that time. She looked up at him, fighting the urge to stare, and wasn't so sure it was going to work, having Nick as her obstetrician. She remembered Flora's words and promised herself she wouldn't fall for her obstetrician.

Having lunch with Nick yesterday, he with his flash convertible and trendy clothes, and she a single-parent house-sitter with no assets, had shown her how big the distance was between them. It had also shown just how easily he could get under her skin.

She did not have the head space for that.

'Thank you for seeing me so quickly.' Being friends might prove a little dangerous but she owed him at least that for being so kind to her.

He settled behind his desk and opened her file. 'You're welcome. I know you're on your way to work.' He glanced at her clothes. 'And need to get changed as well.'

Yeah, well, that had been a non-starter. 'I was trying to be discreet but that failed dismally when I ran into Dr Richards.'

His face softened and she knew he got that. 'If you're worried about people finding out, Callie won't say anything. But it's going to happen soon. Just remember it will all blow over.'

Yeah well. 'It's fine. I was being silly. I'm not ashamed, I just don't want to answer a lot of questions and talk about stuff I haven't had much time to think about. I've told Sister May, anyway. She was the only one I'd worry about finding out from someone else other than me.'

'What about your mother? I meant to ask yesterday. Have you told her about your pregnancy?'

He saw the look that crossed her face, and the intensity of it shocked him. He hadn't picked that up yesterday. He had thought she was safer behind the wall she'd built than she really was.

He wanted to find Lucy's mother and shake her. But as he watched, the look faded and Lucy lifted her chin.

Lucy did not want to think about her mother. It had swamped her for a moment when Nick had asked. She hated sympathy, it always made her want to weep, and she wasn't doing that here.

It was nice he cared but what was her mother to him? 'Yes. But I haven't spoken to her since. I'm not in the mood for a lecture and it's not like listening to her rage is going to change my life.'

He sat back and studied her. She tried not to squirm. 'So how are you feeling in yourself?'

'Still great.' She nodded and glanced at her watch. 'So, did the blood tests all come back okay?'

Nick pushed his less-than-professional questions

away. What was he doing anyway? He should be going through the motions. A normal antenatal visit. Not thinking about yesterday. Not thinking about it really hard.

And she was impatient to be gone. So typically Lucy. He should have guessed from the first morning she'd herded him into Sally's birth unit. No beating around the bush. She was a bit driven, like Callie Richards, and he'd always admired Callie.

The difference was that Lucy refreshed him and he didn't know why. 'The tests were, on the whole, fine. You're a little low with your haemoglobin, so taking iron tablets won't go amiss. Your white cells are a little elevated, so I just wanted to check you're not feeling the effects of any symptoms of infection.'

Her ponytail flipped from side to side. 'Nope. Since yesterday morning I've never felt better.'

Nick smiled and he remembered her appetite from the restaurant. He smiled. 'The second trimester of pregnancy is often the most enjoyable healthwise.'

Lucy reminded herself that she was going to be thankful for everything. 'I'm determined to enjoy it.'

'Good on you. Hold that plan.' He stood up and glided the BP machine over to her chair. 'That sounded patronising but I was sincere. I see a lot of women who expect to be really ill, for some reason, like their mother was, and not surprisingly they are.'

When Nick leaned towards her she could smell that aftershave he'd worn yesterday and she was transported back to sitting with him in his car.

The aftershave had been part of that lovely drive to the beach with him. The whole lovely morning.

But this was now. She watched his big hands wrap the blood-pressure cuff around her arm and pump it up, and she tried not to think about his fingers on her skin.

Before he put the stethoscope into his ears he murmured, 'I just wonder if some women subconsciously programme their bodies to suffer more than they need to.'

She concentrated on his words. Intensely, so she didn't think about his hands. 'Interesting idea and guaranteed to stir up a hornet's nest of debate. My mother hadn't even noticed she was pregnant until too late.'

Déjà vu, then, she thought, and closed her mouth.

That will teach you to stop rabbiting on when he was trying to listen. She kept forgetting he was the senior consultant and she was a new grad midwife—but he was so easy to talk to.

'It's not silly.' He let the blood-pressure cuff all the way down and entered the result on the computer, as well as writing it on the yellow antenatal card he'd started. 'Blood pressure's normal.'

She looked at the card. Something she'd seen so many times held by pregnant women in antenatal clinics everywhere. Funny how something simple like that could bring it all home to her. She was going to have her own babies. 'I'm going to get my own yellow card with my whole pregnancy documented. I never thought I'd have one of those so soon.'

'Yep.' He smiled. 'Don't lose it.'

As if she would. 'Do many women lose their pregnancy records?'

He shook his head. 'No. It's funny really. They lose scripts, ultrasound requests forms, consult letters, but even the dottiest of my patients knows where her card is. I think of it as the first maternal instinct.'

Lucy grinned. 'That's pretty cool, actually.'

'I think so.' He gestured towards the couch with a smile and she knew he was remembering the first sight of her babies up there with his portable ultrasound. Not something she would forget either.

When she'd climbed up onto the couch she pulled up her shirt and they both looked at her belly. It seemed a lot bigger already.

She chewed her lip as she lay down. 'Lucky I wear scrubs at work to hide this.'

He smiled. 'Soon it won't matter what you wear because these little people are going to pop out in front for everyone to see.'

Nick felt above her belly button and gradually moved the heel of his hand down until he felt the firm edge of her uterus. 'You're already above the level of eighteen weeks.'

'Is that good?'

'Expected to be a little over dates.' He slid the little ultrasound Doppler across her belly and they heard one of the baby's heartbeats and then to the left the other one for a brief few seconds. They both smiled. 'We're very lucky to have found them both. It's hit and miss this early to find a single pregnancy heartbeat unless you're using the full ultrasound machine.'

It was incredible how warm and excited just hearing her babies made her feel. Like Christmas was coming. Along with the most expensive credit-card bill yet when she finished work.

He helped her climb down and she could feel the leashed strength under his fingers. There was a funny little knot in her stomach as their hands parted. Uh-oh. She stood on the scales so he could write down her weight and surreptitiously wiped her palm down her jeans.

She looked down at the digital readout. 'I've put on a kilo!'

'I'll mention that to your obstetrician.' They smiled at each other, both remembering Sunday's conversation about ballooning in pregnancy.

She stepped off the scale and sat down again in the chair, and he entered the weight in his computer. 'Everything looks fine.'

'Good.' She glanced at her watch. She had plenty of time to get changed.

'Excellent. Then I'll just send you for a formal ultrasound towards twenty weeks and I'll see you after that. If you have any problems or concerns, you can contact me on this number or just ask if you see me.'

She took his card and glanced at where he'd written his mobile phone number in bold numbers across the back.

'Thank you.' Did he do that for all his women? Not like she could ask. She slipped it into the back of her purse. So it was over. She was back to being just a little new midwife on the ward. Well, that was a good thing.

Nick felt he'd let her down in some way but he couldn't think how so he went back to impersonal mode. Lucy was the same as any other pregnant patient of his. 'You're welcome. Just ask my secretary for an appointment in four weeks.'

He imagined the changes that would happen between now and then. She would be over halfway. She'd be able to feel her babies move. He'd always been fascinated by that.

He watched her jump up. No gentle, ladylike rising for Lucy. Always in a hurry and usually with a smile. He admired her coping ability very much.

'I'll do that.'

'Have a good shift, Lucy.'

The next two weeks passed and Lucy went to her ultrasound appointment when she was just under twenty weeks pregnant with the surprise support person of Flora May.

Flora's enthusiasm was such a pleasure. They smiled with mutual excitement as the ultrasonographer pointed out legs and arms and movements. The babies jiggled about with every move of the ultrasound wand, and Flora laughed and said, 'They'll be a handful.'

Once she'd found out about Lucy's predicament Flora had proved to be her greatest champion, without molly-coddling her.

Unlike Lucy's mother, who'd had only negative comments to offer when Lucy had steeled herself to call, Flora had useful tips and hints on some of the common and less comfortable aspects of pregnancy.

Uncharacteristically, Flora had also quizzed her on how she liked Nick as her doctor, and Lucy had been a bit flustered about that under Flora's knowing gaze.

Coincidentally or not, she'd found herself looking after patients who weren't under the care of Dr Kefes and it actually became easier not having to see Nick all the time because the last thing she needed on top of everything else was a crush on a man who was just being kind.

Nick saw very little of Lucy despite a small unobtrusive effort to keep an eye on her. He found himself thinking often about how Lucy's mother had hurt her.

He could see the shame and hurt of abandonment— it was exactly how Chloe had looked all those years ago when he'd had to tell her their parents hadn't asked about her. Chloe was still affected by the things she'd done because she'd thought she'd had to for their parents' approval. What a disaster that had been.

Initially he'd thought Lucy a confident and independent young woman. She'd certainly made a strong stand on her first shift, but, in fact, he suspected she was vulnerable, and that underneath that bravado she was insecure. That had changed the way he looked at her. Pregnant and fragile, she needed someone to keep an eye on her.

So when he did his morning rounds he tried to check on her, but lately she seemed to melt into the background, and at the end of the day, when he'd taken to visiting the ward one more time before his afternoon appointments, he only caught glimpses of her in the distance.

He was starting to wish he'd made that next antenatal appointment a bit closer, but the latest guidelines were leaning heavily towards fewer visits, not more, for pregnant women, and he didn't want to draw attention to her.

She still hadn't told anyone else except Flora and he was surprised the gossip mill hadn't found out and run with the news. When it did he hoped he was around to make sure she was okay.

In fact, Nick was there when it broke. He rounded the corner just as the night-shift midwife passed the news to the oncoming staff.

'Did you know Flora May's little pet is pregnant? No boyfriend. And twins! What sort of mother will she be?' The words hung in the air as Nick approached and both young women shut their mouths as Nick descended on them.

He actually needed to count to ten before he said

something because what he wanted to say would have caused a much bigger furore than just the announcement. 'Gossiping again, Cass?' He shook his head. 'You'll get a name for it.'

The blonde flushed with embarrassment but Nick was still trying to control his protective reaction. 'By the way, I'm not happy with the observations in birth room one either. Can you do them again before you go off? I'll drop by and check them in the chart later.' He glanced over both women without smiling. 'Thank you.'

He walked away, still fuming, and didn't see Flora May step out of her office into his path.

'Excuse me, Dr Kefes?'

Nick stopped. He refocused, not sure why he was so upset. Focused on Flora. 'Yes?'

Flora watched his face and he tried to lose any expression that would give away his thoughts. 'Do you have a problem with my staff?'

Did he? He was calming down now. He blinked and let his breath out. 'No. Of course not.'

Flora nodded. 'I didn't think so.'

Nick nodded and prepared to move on. Maybe head back to his office to think about what he'd just over-reacted about.

'And, Dr Kefes?'

'Yes?'

'Most people are supportive.'

'Good.'

On the Sunday morning, four weeks after her last appointment, the sun was beating down and Lucy was using the leaf blower to clear the path down to the fence that backed onto the beach.

The blower seemed heavier than last week and her

back ached a little and she wished the palm trees gave her a little more shade. She knew she had to be careful because her body was designed to stretch but there was increased risk of pulling a muscle or over-stretching a ligament thanks to the pregnancy hormones.

She could imagine Flora May saying, 'When you have twins there is even more pregnancy hormone and you have to be careful.'

So she stopped, leaned on the gate in front of the beach, looked over the fence towards the waves and just breathed in the salt-laden air. Her backache eased and the breeze helped. As she began to feel better, she tried to ignore the little skip to her breathing when she thought about seeing Nick tomorrow.

Tried to bring down her silly euphoria by reminding herself her days off were nearly over and the new week ready to begin. Could she do this for another three months?

At least everyone knew she was pregnant now. It was too hard to hide even with the baggy scrub uniform, and Maternity was the best place to work when you were having a baby yourself because it was the place with the least germs.

There'd been a few snide comments, mostly originating from Cass, but a lot of unexpected support from others. Especially Flora May.

She'd be okay. Nick would make sure of that, her inner voice said with a shimmy.

A tall paddleboard rider lifted his hand and waved and instinctively she waved back. Now even the board riders looked like Nick. She needed to settle before tomorrow.

She glanced back at the rider and gulped when the

unknown man turned the board towards her and rode the next wave to the beach opposite her fence.

Good grief, she thought as she watched him pull his board onto the sand, and was about to beat a hasty retreat when she realised that it really *was* Nick.

Nick couldn't believe his luck. He'd known it would be a good idea to buy this board. He trod through the hot sand up to her gate. 'Morning, Lucy.'

Lucy leant on the fence. 'Morning, Nick. I thought I'd accidentally given the come-on to a stray surfer for a minute there.'

He was surprisingly glad she hadn't waved at a stray surfer. He'd known exactly whom he was waving at.

She was dressed in red and green, vibrant like one of the lorikeets feeding off the bottlebrush, but her face was strangely pale. 'Sorry if I scared you.' He wondered if she'd guessed he'd been looking out for her.

'All good. So, what made you paddle by?'

He glanced down at the board under his arm. 'To show off my new toy, and see how you are.'

She gave his board a thorough inspection. 'Your board is very sleek and...dark.'

It had been the best one he could buy. 'I've got a thing for black.'

'I noticed.' She glanced pointedly at his bare feet and raised her brows as if to say, 'Where are your socks?' 'And as for how I am, won't you see me tomorrow?'

He ignored the tomorrow comment and looked a bit closer. 'You look a little tired.'

Her brows shot up. 'You should know women hate being told that!'

'You still look good.' She did, but she wasn't her usual robust self.

'I got hot. Probably need a drink, actually. The owners are coming down tonight and I'm sprucing up the house. Don't want to get kicked out. Especially now.'

He frowned. She did too much. Days off were for her to rest. 'Want a hand? You don't need to work every day.'

Lucy looked at Nick, semi-naked, barefoot, with an extremely cumbersome board hooked under his arm like it was a matchstick, and thought about having him follow her around while she tidied.

It would be much, much easier on her own. And she still felt that little thrill his comment had left her with about looking good. That had been unexpected.

So it wasn't sensible to invite him in, and she was practising sensible. 'Thanks, but, no, thanks.'

She could see Nick hadn't expected the knock-back. She watched him try his special, come-on smile—she'd bet that usually got him the response he wanted. 'I may look like a distinguished obstetrician, but I can mow, trim and clean gutters.'

She could feel a smile inside growing with his determination to get her to change her mind. He was like a stubborn little boy who wanted to play.

'Luckily, I'm not responsible for any of those things, but thanks for the offer.'

She could see that had not been the response he wanted. In fact, he'd crashed and burned, and she watched him assimilate that.

Safety sucked but she needed to stick to her guns.

'The last thing I want is to be a nuisance.'

'As if you could.'

He shrugged easily. 'No problem. I'll see you tomorrow.' He picked up his board and turned back to the sea.

She couldn't believe she'd given the most gorgeous guy she knew the brush-off. But it had been the right thing to do. Depressed, she picked up the blower and her back reminded her it was heavy.

Maybe she should have taken up his offer. She flicked a wistful glance his way but she could see his strong thighs as he strode towards the water and the bulge in his biceps as he carried the board back towards the waves. It was too late. It was actually hard, watching him walk away.

Unexpectedly she felt a strange cramp low at the front of her abdomen and her annoying backache took on a more sinister significance. What if it wasn't just the heaviness of the leaf blower?

Then she realised her babies hadn't moved much that morning, and a deep unease expanded in her chest.

When the cramp came back, this time intensified into a painful drag in her belly, she had to drop the blower and clutch at the fence.

'Nick,' she said in a small scared little voice. Not surprisingly, he couldn't hear because he was almost into the waves. She edged towards the gate and opened it as if her voice would carry further. She just needed the pain to stop so she could call out.

To Lucy's intense relief, before he climbed onto his board, Nick looked back and waved. She waved, signalled him back, a little frantically, and he stopped.

Stared at her.

She saw him tilt his head as if wondering if he'd misunderstood. The pain came again and she put both hands on the fence.

When she looked up Nick was through the gate and beside her. His board was halfway up the sand where he'd dropped it. All she could think was how good it was he'd come back.

The concern in his voice made her eyes sting. 'You okay?'

'I'm not sure.' Her voice cracked.

Nick saw the tears at the corners of her eyes. What was this all about? Somewhere inside a voice mocked him, told him to watch out, and he panicked that she was getting needy for him. He did not do needy.

Then she said the unexpected. 'I've had a few cramps in my back this morning and thought it was because I was carrying the blower. But now they've moved to the front.' Big worry-flecked eyes searched his face for reassurance.

What?

All thoughts of himself disappeared.

She chewed her lip. 'I'm scared it's the babies.'

His mind went blank except for the big words, 'miscarriage', 'prem labour', and they were suddenly unpalatable thoughts. She'd be twenty-two weeks.

That was too early for the babies to have a fighting chance. He didn't ask himself how it was he knew exactly how far along she was. But instinctively he stepped in, gathered her against him and his arms went around her.

Surprisingly she fitted into his body like a jigsaw piece he'd always been missing and he soaked in the warmth of her as if he'd been chilled.

'It's okay,' he murmured into her hair as he breathed in the scent of herbs and spring and Lucy.

He squeezed her gently. His hand came up and smoothed her hair and he suddenly connected with what he was doing and his relationship force field snapped back into place. He did not do emotional.

He loosened his arms. Stepped back.

Steered her to the wrought-iron seat while his mind beat him up with reminders not to get involved.

'Sit. Take it easy. It might be nothing.' He hoped it was nothing.

He hadn't picked the amount of investment he had in these babies already. He needed to snap out of that and get back to the person with the medical degree. 'Have you had any bleeding?'

'Not that I know of.' She'd wrapped her arms around her lower belly, protecting her children, and it did strange things to his chest to see her so panicked.

Distress vibrated off her in bigger waves than those in the nearby ocean.

She sat as directed, as if it would all be all right if she did everything she was told, as if he held her fate in his hands. No pressure. Not.

'Okay. No bleeding. That's good. It might have just been a warning sign for you to take it a little easier. Have you any pain now?'

She shook her head and her hair fell into her eyes. He resisted the urge to brush it back.

'Just a tiny ache in my back.'

Her back. Still suspicious. 'Is it coming and going or there all the time?'

'There all the time.'

Best of the bad. 'Again, that's good. Maybe you have a low-grade kidney infection. Very common with pregnant women and a big player in causing premature labour.'

He saw her wince when he said it but she needed to know he wasn't joking. Maybe he should have tested her again for infections, even though she'd said she was fine.

There was that raised white cell count. He didn't stop

to ask why he was beating himself up about something he would have done for anyone else. But this was Lucy.

Lucy was in shock. From two things—the stark terror of risk to her babies and the absolute comfort she'd gained from being wrapped up in Nick's arms. All that salty skin and muscle around her had felt like a shield from the world.

As if nothing in the universe could go wrong as long as she was snuggled into his arms. So it had been a nasty reality when he'd disentangled himself and sat her away from him.

Now he expected her to take in what he was saying when her mind felt like she was inside a big ball of cotton wool and danger was waiting if she peeked out.

'Sorry?' She concentrated and the cotton wool thinned a little. 'Kidney infection?'

Yep, maybe. She had been dashing for the ladies more often this week. She should have picked that up. They could fix that. Everything would be okay if she took it easy until antibiotics sorted that irritation.

Maybe she'd take Monday off. Thank goodness she'd told Flora May about the pregnancy. And Nick could take her aside and explain as well. Or was that presuming too much?

He glanced up towards the house. 'You go to bed. I'll write you a script. In fact, I'll get the antibiotics from the chemist for you. We'll get a sample from you before you take your first dose so we can make sure we've targeted the right bug.'

Lucy listened to him laying out the strategy and she couldn't help thanking whatever lucky stars had directed Nick to paddle past her door today. She had no idea what she would have done if he hadn't been around. And she'd sent him away.

'I'll get my sister to bring a sterile container from work for the specimen. She's at work this morning and she won't mind dropping in.'

Lucy's stomach sank. She hadn't met Nick's sister. What would she think about a pregnant junior midwife latching onto her brother and asking for family favours?

Cringe factor of ten. 'It's okay. I can get one of the girls from work to do that.'

Nick shook his head decisively. Not the easygoing Nick, this was the consultant—Dr Kefes, Nick. 'Too much organising when you're going to bed to rest. I'll sort this.' He looked past her. 'Where's your place?'

'Down behind the pool.'

'Do you want me to carry you?'

Oh, my word, she could picture it. Feel his arms. 'No. I'll be fine.'

'You sure?'

Sob. 'Yep, sure.' She stood up and the pain was there at the back but the front was okay at the moment.

Nick followed her closely along the narrow path, as if she was going to faint or something.

Halfway down the path the contraction pain came again and this time she really got scared. She stopped and swayed and then his arms came around her gently and he pulled her back against his chest.

'I've got you.'

Then he lifted her—like she wasn't a tall girl with two passengers, but a tiny wisp of nothing—and cradled her against his chest, but sadly she was too focused on the grinding ache low in her belly to enjoy the ride.

CHAPTER FIVE

NICK PUSHED OPEN the screen with his shoulder and angled Lucy through the door still in his arms. She pointed to her little room that had come furnished, all designer white cane furniture with hibiscus quilt and pillow covers and Hawaiian surf photos, and he carried her through.

When he put her down, tears threatened and stung her eyes but she was darned if she was going to let them fall—while he was here anyway. 'I'm fine.'

'Mmm-hmm.' He glanced around. 'Much more of this and I'll admit you to the hospital.'

Too real and scary. 'Seriously. It's gone now.'

He narrowed his eyes at her. 'So that pain was in the front?'

'Yep.' She looked at him, dwarfing her little room, so out of place amongst the white doilies and spindly cane. 'But I'll rest.'

'I'll go to the chemist.' He glanced at his watch. Calculating which chemist would be open probably. 'But I'll have to go home first. Is it okay if I go out the road entrance?' He was so full of purpose. She wasn't used to people taking control. Being a back-up for her. It felt dangerously good, and she needed to snap out of it.

'Sure. The gate will lock behind you.' She reached

onto her bedside table and gave him her keys. 'Use these to get back in. The blue key is for the gate.' She consoled herself that he wouldn't listen anyway if she said she'd be fine on her own.

He glanced back into the other room—lounge, kitchen, dining all in one—and focused on the fridge. 'You look like the kind of girl who keeps bottles of water in the fridge.'

He crossed the room in a few steps and peered into the refrigerator. 'Knew it.' She had to smile as he grabbed a pink plastic drink bottle, picked up her mobile phone from the table, and put them beside her bed.

He pointed his finger at her. 'Stay!'

She sank back on the pillows and to be honest it felt good not to be standing up. 'Yes, sir.' Yes, sir?

He raised his brows. 'Now she gets cheeky. Ring me if you need me.'

'Thanks, Nick.' He was such a hero. But not her hero. The tears got closer.

His face softened and she needed him to go. Now. 'Thank me later,' he said, and left.

Nick frowned at himself as he trod back to the beach entrance, hopped down onto the sand and picked up his paddleboard and paddle. As he locked the gate and retraced his steps past her little bungalow he berated himself. Thank me later? What was that? Asking for a what? A kiss? Get a grip.

The driveway gate clanged shut behind him as he set off along the road for his flat. The board and paddle were bulky and a nuisance under his arm. The path was hot under his bare feet and her keys felt strange in his other hand.

He was getting way too involved here. If he wasn't

careful there'd be emotion involved and he didn't want to go there. He knew where that led. To people being able to stamp on you when you were at your weakest. No way was he going there. But what could he do? She didn't seem to have a friend in the world. He was here. What else could he do? He'd ring Chloe when he got home.

Chloe wasn't as supportive as he'd hoped she'd be. His sister didn't take it lightly. 'So she's a patient?'

What was with the suspicion? 'Yeah. But she's a friend. A colleague.'

There was a definite worried tinge in her voice. What was with that? 'She's your patient, though. You're caring for her during her pregnancy?'

He'd already answered that. 'Yes. She's a midwife on the ward.'

He could hear the frown in her voice. 'It's not like you to become involved. Be careful, Nick.'

Nick lifted the phone away from his ear. He did not want to hear this. He put it back. 'Hell, Chloe. Just get me the container and drop it off here when you come home.'

There was a pause. Then, 'I finish work in twenty minutes.'

'Thank you.' He disconnected and threw the phone on the bed. Stripped off his board shorts and trod across to the shower.

Sisters. When had he ever tried to tell her what to do? He paused with his hand on the tap.

Maybe a couple of times, or more if he was being honest, but that didn't give her the right to go jumping to conclusions about him and Lucy.

He turned the cold tap on with controlled force and stepped underneath the spray. Sucked his breath in and forced himself to stand there.

Not that he needed to have a cold shower because he was thinking about Lucy, but it was hot outside. And he wanted to get back to her as soon as he could. He hoped she wasn't going to miscarry her babies.

He'd been going to wait for Chloe to come first before heading out to the chemist's but if he got a wriggle on he reckoned he could get there and back before she finished work. Then he could go straight to Lucy's.

He hoped to hell she didn't get stronger contractions. As long as she didn't bleed it looked okay. Antibiotics should take care of the irritation and with a little rest she'd be fine. Her babies would be fine.

He'd see if he could do something practical in the yard for her or she'd be lying there worrying that the house wasn't perfect for the owners. No. She didn't want help. She was too independent.

He turned the water off and grabbed the towel. Dried himself quickly and dragged on underwear, some shorts and a shirt.

Lucy's crisis had taken over his day and he didn't stop to think why this threatened miscarriage was any different from the dozens he'd dealt with in the past.

During his time when he'd mostly concentrated on IVF, dealing with bereaved parents had been a part of almost every day, and his own sadness had been one of the reasons he didn't do as much of that these days. But this was different.

He grabbed his wallet and keys and a script pad and pen. It would be fine. He could deal with this.

Back at her house Lucy told herself she was starting to feel better.

What more could she ask for? If she'd gone into the emergency department there was nothing they could do for her except what Nick was doing. And that would be after a long wait in the waiting room.

She was only just pregnant enough for it to be noticeable in the obstetric ward. They probably wouldn't even have done an ultrasound unless she bled.

That had been the first thing she'd done when Nick had left. She'd jumped up and checked she wasn't bleeding. The relief that she wasn't had been immeasurable.

So if she'd gone to the hospital all anyone could have done would have been to check for an infection that could be irritating her body into contractions, treat any infection that was there, and send her home to rest. She didn't want to think about what would happen if she progressed into full premature labour.

It would be termed a tragic loss of an unviable twin pregnancy. They'd tell her to hang on for another week. As if she wouldn't do anything to hang on.

Her abdomen tightened ominously and she sucked in her breath and forced herself to breathe out. Be loose. Be relaxed. Don't get stressed.

She tried to swallow the lump lodged in her throat. Even the wonders of medical science couldn't help her babies if they were born. Dreadful odds for a healthy outcome.

In the last few weeks she hadn't even contemplated losing them. 'Very premature birth' were three terrifying words. Why would she have thought this could happen?

She stroked her tight little mound gently and sniffed back the tears. 'Come on, babies. Stop frightening your mummy.'

She had the top obstetrician in the hospital looking after her, at her home, sending off samples, procuring her antibiotics, all without her having to leave the comfort of her bed. And without the whole hospital rampant with curiosity.

Maybe Nick was right, and she just needed to be more careful. Had she been doing too much in the garden? Or maybe she shouldn't have reached up for those overhanging fronds?

Guilt swamped her and it didn't help that she knew, rationally, she hadn't done anything wrong. 'I'm so sorry, babies,' she whispered.

As if in answer a tiny knee or elbow rose in her stomach and poked her as if to reassure her. She smiled mistily. It was incredible, the bond she felt to these tiny pods of humanity who had slipped into her heart so unexpectedly. Her whole life was affected by their now planned-for arrival in around four months' time and she realised, far too belatedly, that she'd be devastated if she lost them.

She looked imploringly at the ceiling. 'I promise I'll be more careful, God. Honest.' A tear trickled down her cheek.

'If I can just keep my babies.' She glanced around the room, feeling slightly guilty with the fact that she only thought of praying when she wanted something. And she hadn't realised how much she really wanted these babies.

A knock on the door had her reach for a tissue and she blew her nose just as Nick poked his head in. 'How are you doing?'

As he approached the bed Nick saw the traces of tears on her cheeks and her eyes were suspiciously bright. But her voice was normal so he hoped nothing too catastrophic had happened while he'd been away. He put down the backpack he'd brought stuff in.

'You okay?' She looked damp but tragically beautiful. It was the first time he'd thought of her as beautiful, didn't know why he hadn't seen it before. But it wasn't helpful in this situation.

'I'm fine.' She sniffed and sat up straighter. Squared her shoulders and smiled bravely. 'And no bleeding.'

'Good.' Relief warmed his belly. 'Let's keep it that way.' He lifted out the paper bag his sister had given him and the packet of antibiotics he'd picked up. 'Start the antibiotics as soon as you visit the bathroom.'

He saw her blush and he knew that she felt embarrassed about all this. But it all needed to be done and done properly.

'I brought you a mini-quiche and a yoghurt, in case you were hungry.' He took them from the bag, too. It had seemed a good idea at the time but now he felt a bit dumb about it. She was in her own home and of course she'd have food in the refrigerator.

She didn't look like she thought it was dumb. 'Thank you. That's very kind. And I just ran out of yoghurt.'

He handed her the yoghurt. 'It's acidophilus. Always a good idea if you're on antibiotics.'

She frowned and then her face cleared as he guessed she got the homeopathic connection of antibiotics and yeast infections and the natural fighting abilities of acidophilus. Because she laughed.

He wasn't sure if it was a good thing to be laughed at for thinking about things like that but he was a gynaecologist, too. He actually saw the tension fall from her face and decided it was a good thing even if it was at his expense.

She grinned at him. 'Not a lot of girls get that kind of service.'

'Well, you're special.' And she was. But just because she didn't have anybody else and she did still remind him of the sort of support Chloe should have had when she'd had her teen pregnancy. Not that Lucy was a teen. Far from it, but it explained the affinity he felt with her. And the fact that he knew she was more vulnerable than she let on.

'Thank you, kind sir.' She looked past him to the kitchen. 'Did you want a cup of tea or anything?'

'Nope.' He paused. 'Look. I know I've already asked but things are a little different now. If you rest up here, is there anything you really need me to do outside before the owners come?'

He thought she was going to refuse again, but saw the tiny hesitation. 'Come on. Spit it out.'

Her cheeks were pink and he could see she hated to ask. It seemed he needn't have worried she'd abuse his help. Not that he'd really thought she would, but Chloe had mentioned it again, and he mentally poked his tongue out at his suspicious sister.

'I left the blower down by the beach gate. Could I ask you to put it back in the garden shed for me, please?' She chewed her lip and he wanted to ask her not to do that. It made him feel uncomfortable.

He nodded. 'I'll do that and poke around to see if there's anything obvious to tidy up then I'll be back. Don't stress if I take a while. Do you have a computer here?'

'No, unfortunately. It's getting fixed.'

'I brought my tablet computer if you want to go online and search the web.' He reached into the backpack and withdrew it.

'Wow.' She peered over the edge of the bed and pointed to his pack. 'Mary Poppins, eat your heart out. What else have you got in there? Maybe a lampshade and an umbrella?'

He didn't get it. A lampshade? Why would he want an umbrella? 'Who's Mary Poppins?'

She grinned and he had to smile back. She had a great smile. 'Didn't you watch Disney movies when you were a kid?' She smiled. 'My mother was always going out and I was left with a big pile of Disney movies to keep me company.'

He really wasn't liking the sound of her childhood. But, then, his had been the opposite. Too strict. 'Disney must have been too commercial. Not on our Orthodox parents' video list.' He glanced at the almost empty bag. 'Nothing much left in there.'

He didn't want to tell her he had a Doppler for listening to foetal heartbeats because he didn't really want to go there. He wasn't quite sure why he'd brought it. Maybe just for his own peace of mind in case she asked.

'I'll just slip out and sort the blower. Take the antibiotics as soon as you can, won't you?'

She blushed again. It was kind of cute the way she did that. 'Yep. Will do.'

Nick blinked and stepped back. Whoa. Stop that thought. 'Right. I'll sort outside, then.' He spun and headed for the door like the hounds of hell were after him. Maybe Chloe wasn't so dumb after all and he did need to be careful.

By the time he'd used the blower around the pool, fished out some palm fronds and cleaned the filter box, he decided he'd devoted enough of his Sunday to Lucy. But when he went back to say goodbye she was asleep.

And he couldn't leave until he made sure she and her babies were okay.

So he sat down beside her bed on the spindly cane chair and watched her sleep.

Once she mumbled, as if talking to someone, and her

hand drifted to her belly as she smiled the softest, gentlest smile, and it tore unexpectedly at the wall he'd built so successfully around his heart so many years ago.

When she rested her hand over the babies inside her he had to stifle the urge to reach across, lay his hand over hers and feel what she was feeling, assure himself these tiny beings who had somehow pierced his armour were healthy and happy.

Instead, he reminded himself that this family was not his family—and they needed someone with a heart to give, not someone moulded by callous parents who could cast off their children without a backward glance.

Nikolai forced his eyes away and checked his email. Browsed the web. Closed his eyes.   .

When Lucy woke up, Nick was asleep in the chair beside her bed.

Was this guy for real? She'd never had anyone care about her like he had. Except maybe Lil and Clem next door, when she'd been a kid and had got lonely while her mother had been out.

Which reminded her, she needed to let the kind older couple know how she was doing. They were thrilled she had twins coming. Had promised her all manner of equipment they'd finished with. They'd had their own IVF twins the year before she'd moved out and started her training. They'd understand about twins. But that was for after all this worry went away.

She felt her belly and it seemed softer than before. There were no pains in her back or low in her belly. Maybe it was all going to be okay anyway. She hoped so. When she looked back at Nick he had woken up and was watching her. He smiled and she smiled back.

'Hey, sleepyhead,' she said.

'Hey, sleepyhead, yourself. I was on my way out

and your snoring was so loud I thought I'd better wait till you woke up.'

As if. 'I do not snore.'

'So I've found out.' He smiled at her. 'And you look better. Less tense.'

She gently touched her belly. 'And no pain that I know of.'

He stood up and the chair creaked a little. She had to smile. 'That's great. I still think you should have tomorrow off.'

She'd been thinking that, too. 'It scared me. I'll do whatever you recommend, Nick.'

'I'll talk to Sister May. You've still got my number?'

She nodded and he picked up his backpack and the paper bag she'd left there for him. He raised his brows as he picked it up, checking she'd done the deed, and she nodded.

Her ears felt hot. 'I tightened the lid as tight as I could get it.'

He grinned. 'Good.' He slid his tablet in after the paper bag and zipped up the rucksack. 'Ring me any time and I'll drop in if you need me. Or even if you just have a question. It's okay, Lucy. You can ring me and if it's not a good time I'll have my phone on silent and will ring you back. Okay?'

She nodded. 'Otherwise I'll see you for our appointment tomorrow.'

That was good. They could do another check. 'Why don't I arrange for you to have another scan beforehand? We can compare it to the one you had two weeks ago. That way you can be sure everything is fine.'

She'd been going to ask him for that. Her shoulders dropped with relief. 'Thanks. That would be good.'

'I'll ring you with a time when I find out tomorrow.

See you then,' he said, and she could tell he wanted to get going.

Of course he did. The poor guy had had his whole Sunday hijacked by her and she felt terrible. And special. He'd said she was special but she'd better not get any ideas.

Because she didn't want to get all gooey and mushy over a certain obstetrician, one who probably thought of her as the biggest nuisance out, because no man would want to hook up with a pregnant, single mother of twins.

But seriously! What wasn't there to love about Nikolai Kefes?

The guy had created calm out of her sudden plunge into uncertainty, had tidied up the outside of her house-sitting mansion so she wouldn't feel like she'd let the owners down, and had even run to the chemist's and now the pathology department for her.

But in reality the last thing she needed was a broken heart to carry along with two babies, because even a twin stroller wouldn't be big enough to carry all that.

So she definitely wasn't going there.

CHAPTER SIX

NICK HAD RUNG to say Lucy's new ultrasound appointment was at twelve o'clock and as she dressed, she wondered who was missing out on their lunch to do the favour for Nick.

When she was shown into the little room and directed to climb up on the couch in her patient gown, the bombshell blonde ultrasonographer, a different technician from last time, wasn't behind in letting her know. 'Dr Kefes wouldn't take no for an answer so let's see why these babies of yours are causing him such concern.'

As she dimmed the lights there was a knock on the door and BB opened it to Nick. 'Hello, there, Nikolai.' She laughed and signalled for him to come in. 'I wondered if you'd show up for this.'

Lucy blinked at the familiarity in her tone and couldn't help wondering if these two had been more than just professional colleagues. Not that it was any of her business.

'Hi, Jacqui. Thanks for this. I owe you one.' Nick followed the woman into the small room, which suddenly became much smaller, and Lucy didn't like the way he smiled back at the technician. Not that she even had the right to notice who Nick looked at.

Jacqui seemed pretty happy. 'Oh, goody. Dinner.'

He grinned and nodded at Lucy. 'How are you, Lucy? No more pain?'

'I'm fine, thanks.' Except for this ridiculous feeling of exclusion she should not be feeling. An exclusion she had no right to complain about when Nick and Jacqui were both going out of their way to help her. She was an ungrateful wretch.

And they were going out to dinner.

'So let's see what these kids are up to.' Jacqui tilted the screen so Lucy, and now Nick, could see the pictures, and thankfully Lucy could concentrate on the still unfamiliar excitement of actually outlining the shapes of her babies. Thankfully, everything else disappeared from her mind.

With the extra power of the large machine, Lucy could even see their little faces. Could hear and watch the chambers of their hearts all moving as they should. Gaze with wonder as a tiny hand clenched and unclenched. Then a tiny leg kicked.

They were so tiny, and fragile, and vulnerable. She could have gone into proper labour yesterday, and with lungs too small to breathe for long they would have been gone today.

An explosion of fear ballooned in her chest and she drew a breath. They were her family. Her babies, who would always love her, and she would always love them. What if she'd lost them?

Nick must have sensed her distress because he drew closer and rested his hand on her shoulder. Pressed down. With his fingers sending reassuring vibes, she could feel her panic subside a little. 'It's okay, Lucy. They look great.'

She tore her eyes from the screen to search his face.

His eyes met hers, intense, reassuring. He nodded. Wordlessly he told her he was telling the truth and she breathed out.

Suddenly exhausted by the fear that had come from nowhere and was so slow to ebb away, she sank back into the pillow. Okay. It was okay. Nick said everything would be fine.

'Good two-week growth from last time. Do you want to know the sex?' Jacqui was intent on the screen and had missed the byplay. Probably a good thing, Lucy thought with a tinge of guilt, judging by the way this hospital picked up scandal.

Nick's hand lifted away but it was okay. Lucy dragged her mind back to what Jacqui had said. Sex? Not sexes? 'Are they identical?'

'It looks like it to me.'

Lucy grinned at that. Identical twins. Awesome, and how cute! And her babies would never be alone because they would have each other. Lucky babies. Did she want to know what sex? 'No. I don't think so. I like the idea of a surprise.'

Jacqui was very good at her job. In no time she'd done all the measurements, estimated both babies' weights and checked all around the edge of the big placenta to see if there was any sign of bleeding or separation.

'Nope. All looks good. Nice amount of fluid around the babies. Good blood flow through both umbilical cords. Nothing out of the ordinary except there's two of them. Measure at twenty-two weeks.' She put the ultrasound handpiece back on its stand and handed Lucy a towel to dry her belly while she concentrated on Nick. 'Satisfied, Dr Kefes?'

'Very. Thank you, Jacqui.' Lucy swiped the jelly off her belly and tried not to look at the way Jacqui leant towards Nick. It was none of her business.

She swung her legs over the edge of the couch but before she could jump down, Nick was there with his hand to help her. 'Can you follow me to my office, Lucy, and I'll chase up the results of those tests?'

She kept her voice upbeat with an effort. 'Great. That saves me waiting till the later appointment.'

'That's fine.' He opened the door for her. 'I'll meet you there in a minute.'

Lucy went past him into the ultrasound waiting room and he shut the door. She wondered with just a tinge of acid just how he was thanking Jacqui until she smacked herself. None of her business.

Whatever appreciation he'd offered, it didn't take long because Nick caught up with her outside the lifts.

Meanwhile, above Nick and Lucy and inside the lift that sailed towards them, Callie Richards ground her teeth, silently but no less effectively as she stewed. Cade Coleman! Grrr.

She could see him in her mind's eye without turning her head. She didn't want to look at him. Dark brown, wavy hair. Those light brown eyes assessing her. Always assessing. Coldly. As if she came up short every time. Well, she wasn't short, she was five feet ten, for heaven's sake, and she was damn good at her job.

This last case had been gruelling. Nick had called them in at three a.m. and it hadn't finished until an hour ago, but by the time she'd spent eight hours trying to ignore Cade Coleman in a room full of people she'd had enough.

Her nerves had been shredded and the worst part was she didn't know why she couldn't just rise above him. Build a bridge. Get over him. All the things that grown-up, footloose women did.

She jumped when he spoke. 'How come you didn't stay long in the recovery room? Those parents will have more questions.'

'Don't tell me my job. I'll go back again later.' She shook her head. 'Soon.'

I just need a few minutes to calm down first, she thought despairingly. If this stupid lift could get its act together and get her to the ground floor before she burst into tears.

She seriously needed sleep. There'd been a long session in the NICU the previous evening and her eyes felt grainy. That was the only reason she was feeling fragile.

'Really?'

She turned her head in time to see him look her up and down and her blood pressure escalated again.

There was censure in his tone. 'I heard you were the real heart of this hospital. Hearts don't leave.'

Oh, yeah? Not that she thought about it much, but her heart had left years ago. And so apparently had his. Even his brother had warned her when he'd suggested Cade for the job.

He'd been the one who'd said that happily ever after wasn't for people like them.

Those words haunted her. If he wasn't interested, why didn't he just leave her alone and stop pushing her buttons?

But he didn't. 'Is this to do with me knocking you back for a dance at the wedding? When you were tipsy?'

Callie winced. Now, that had been a dumb dare from the girls. 'Don't be stupid.' She certainly regretted draping herself all over him but that was why she hadn't had a glass of wine since.

He looked her up and down. 'Because we could make

a date. Dance the night away and more. No strings, no expectations. Get it out of our systems.'

After being an absolute horror to her all night. Was he joking? 'Strangely, I decline.'

He shrugged and she wondered if he was as laid back about it as he looked. 'Have to find someone else, then.'

The doors opened and Cade and Callie moved back against the wall. Callie forced a smile and nodded at the little midwife, Lucy. With Nick again?

She frowned slightly. These two seemed to end up in the same space a fair bit. She glanced at Nick and he barely looked tired, despite the long night.

He grinned at them both. Where did he get his energy? 'Thanks for the big night, guys. You were incredible. The parents are still coming to grips with things and I said you'd see them again later. That right, Callie?'

'Half an hour. Just have to sort something first.'

'Great. That's what I told them.' He glanced at Cade. 'Amazing job, Cade.'

'But tense. I think I need some heavy exercise to get the kinks out of my neck.' He glanced sardonically at Callie and then at Nick. 'You up for a game of squash later, Nick?'

'What time?'

'Six-thirty and I'm going to flog you.' What a poseur, Callie thought as she listened, but Nick didn't seem fazed. She hoped he wiped the floor with Cade.

Nick just smiled. 'Make it seven, and meet your match.'

She gave Lucy a look that said *Men!* and Lucy grinned as the lift stopped and she and Nick got out. 'I need to catch up with you later, too, Nick.' Callie saw Nick pause and he turned back, saluted her, and the lift doors shut.

Cade looked thoughtfully at the closed door. 'You think Nick is having an affair with that girl?'

'No.' She hoped not because she'd heard the girl was pregnant. 'There's enough gossip in this place already, without making up more.'

'Makes me wonder if they sail up and down the lift together all day.'

The lift finally made it to ground level and the doors opened. 'As long as they don't think we are, it's all good,' Callie muttered, and hurried off.

She could feel his eyes drilling into her back and she picked up more speed.

Back on the level of the consultants' rooms, Nick ushered Lucy through the door into his office and Lucy passed the empty secretary's desk. She'd forgotten it was lunchtime for everyone else because she'd arranged this before she'd known she'd be off sick.

Lucy took her usual seat while he opened up the screen for the results and she thought about the conversation in the lift.

They must have all been in Theatre together. He didn't look tired. 'Were you up all night, operating?'

'Half the night. Complicated triplet pregnancy.' He clicked the mouse. 'Ah, here they are. Yep. Right antibiotics for the bug and a probable cause for your irritable uterus.'

Lucy was still thinking about the three babies. Gulp. 'So there's people out there who are more complicated than me.'

'Always. And lots that are simpler. People forget that twins are tricky. With IVF we get a lot more twins and triplets than normal and it's a serious pregnancy we need to keep a close eye on.'

They did the blood-pressure and weight check and skipped the abdominal palpation because the ultrasound had shown them both the babies were growing well. Nick handed back the card he'd filled out. 'Don't hesitate to call me if you have any concerns.'

He was in doctor mode and she needed to remember that's who he was. He was her doctor, not her friend.

She stood up. 'Yes. Thank you. I'd better get home and put my feet up or I'll be feeling guilty I didn't go to work.'

CHAPTER SEVEN

AT THREE-THIRTY that afternoon Flora May dropped by at Lucy's house to check that she was okay. The company was appreciated because Lucy felt strangely flat.

Flora glanced around at the secluded alcove with palm trees overhead and birds flying in and out. 'It's like being on a little tropical island. No wonder you like it here.'

Lucy watched a lorikeet dart past and tried to lift her mood. Yes. She was lucky. It was a great place to live. 'Plus it's rent-free for very little maintenance of the big house. And nice and close to the hospital.'

Actually, Lucy wanted to throw herself on Flora's motherly chest but she'd been stifling those urges since she'd been a little girl. She'd thought she was pretty good at it but lately her reserves seemed to be running low.

She felt Flora's scrutiny. 'How are you, Lucy?'

'I'm fine. Nick arranged for another ultrasound. The babies are fine. We're just being careful.'

Flora's eyes it up. 'So how was the ultrasound? Did they move much? And that was very sensible.' She'd brought a cake and they set up the little table outside Lucy's door.

Lucy remembered that moment when she'd thought

about losing them, and how Nick had reassured her. 'They looked good. Kicking well.' She didn't know what she'd have done without him the last few days but she didn't want to get used to relying on him. It was nice having Flora visit, too. Almost like a family, but who was she kidding? She needed to get better at going it alone, not worse.

Flora poured the tea. 'So when do you think you'll be back at work?'

'Tomorrow.'

'Good.' Flora sat back. 'Dr Kefes is looking after you well?'

Lucy smiled at the question in Flora's voice. As if she would have words with him if he wasn't doing his job well. 'I wouldn't be going tomorrow if he thought it was dangerous.' She could just imagine Flora taking Nick to task for being negligent. 'In fact, he's been great.'

She couldn't tell Flora how great or the rumour mill would go into overdrive. Not that Flora gossiped. That wouldn't be in her psyche, but it could be awkward if Flora thought she and Nick had something going on when, of course, they didn't. 'I'd like you to try and come with me to the next ultrasound if you're not busy?'

Flora's face softened and she smiled. 'I'd like that.'

Flora stayed another hour and then left, but not before Lucy promised to phone in sick if she felt unwell.

She was so glad she'd told Flora, who'd suggested she allow the news to spread so people would understand and be a little more thoughtful in what they asked Lucy to do.

The next day at work Lucy felt as good as new. Maybe it was because she had slept in that morning, and start-

ing work after lunch instead of before breakfast seemed
to suit her better.

The ward was busy, and after checking Lucy was
okay Flora glanced at the clock.

'Right, then.' Back to business. 'I'll get you to care
for Bonny Shore. Her husband can't be here because
they have no one to mind their two toddler daughters.'

'Oh, poor thing.'

'Yes. Meg's in there and I don't think she'll go home
before the birth so the two of you will be there. The
exciting thing is that Bonny's having twins, too.' Flora
smiled and Lucy wanted to give Flora a hug because this
was just what she needed—an insight into the happy
ending of a twin pregnancy.

'The neonatal nursery is aware we're close but ready
to come when we think they'll be needed. Dr Richards
and Dr Coleman have been to see Bonny and explain
that two neonatal teams will be there just in case either
baby decides to be naughty.'

Lucy had to smile at that but inwardly she quailed
at the thought of so many consultants in the room. Especially the terrifying Dr Coleman.

But she'd have to get used to it. This was her world
and she vowed she would become a valuable part of the
network at Gold Coast City Hospital.

Flora went on. 'Of course, Dr Kefes and his registrar
will be there also, so the room will become very busy
when the time comes.

'Until then...' she looked at Lucy from under her
stern brows '...try and give Bonny some reassurance
that despite the cast of thousands she does have some
control over her birth and that she is still doing what
she is designed to do.'

Lucy grinned. 'Absolutely.' She looked up at her mentor. How she wished she'd had someone like this kind woman as her mother or even her aunt. Her dream had been that one day she'd get a warm and fuzzy mother-in-law who would be the kind of mother she'd never had but that dream had slipped further away. He'd have to be some man to want a wife who already had twins.

Maybe that would never happen but Flora was becoming her friend.

'And thank you.' She looked away because her silly hormones were filling her eyes with tears again. 'For caring.'

For a moment Flora's eyes softened and then she looked towards the birthing suites. 'Away you go.'

As Lucy knocked and entered, her patient, Bonny, was shaking her head and pushing the straps off her belly. 'I need to go into the shower.' Her voice cracked. 'I can't sit on this bed any more.'

Bonny Shore was thirty years old, this was her third pregnancy, and she'd had normal births with her two little girls who were waiting at home. By the strained look on Bonny's face, this was all very different.

Lucy suspected her patient was stressed by the extra observations needed for twins, plus she was heading into late active labour.

Lucy had seen that this could be the most challenging time, transition between the first and second stages of labour, before the pushing became compulsive, a time that often left a woman agitated, fearful and sometime quite cross.

As she learnt more each day, Lucy was starting to re-alise that mums needed extra-calm support right about now. She could remember Flora telling her in her train-ing that this was the usual time for women to abuse their husbands, if they weren't at home minding the other children.

Lucy wondered briefly if she would have anyone to be cross at when she had her babies then scolded herself for being self-absorbed and crossed over the room to Meg. The other young graduate midwife looked up from the foetal monitor as Lucy appeared.

They smiled at each other, acknowledging silently the excitement of the impending birth. They both glanced at the two resuscitation cots set up together at the side of the room.

'Well, here's Lucy come to help you into the shower, too,' Meg, said reassuringly. 'This is the midwife I told you about who's expecting twins as well.'

Bonny looked across and rolled her eyes at Lucy. 'Hi, there. And poor you.' She glanced down at her large rounded belly and then suddenly smiled softly. 'And lucky you.'

As they helped Bonny down from the bed, Meg quietly went through her patient's progress. 'Bonny began her contractions this morning at home about six a.m. She came to us at ten, once she had her girls sorted, and was four centimetres dilated already by then.'

'Wow.' Lucy was impressed. 'That was great progress at home.'

'My husband was a mess by the time he dropped me off and I got into trouble from Dr Kefes for not coming earlier.' Bonny grinned as she shuffled across the room towards the bathroom, her hands under the swell of her huge abdomen to support it.

Lucy could tell she was not at all abashed at the scolding. Then the next contraction took hold and they all stopped as Bonny leant against Lucy and breathed through the contraction.

As they stood quietly and gently breathed together, Lucy realised there was no tension in the room, just a feeling of solidarity, and she thought again how lucky she was to have found her niche in life.

The contraction eased and Bonny went on as if she hadn't stopped. 'He listened when I said I didn't want an epidural. Though he did get an intravenous pin in when I didn't want one.'

Bonny looked up under her hair at Lucy. 'Though it's coming to that point in this labour when you tell yourself you'd forgotten how strong it gets.' She pushed forward grimly and held onto the doorpost as the next contraction rolled through, then she sighed again and forced herself to relax.

'Getting to the business end,' Lucy said gently.

'Precisely.' Bonny's eyes were fixed on the shower nozzle as if it was calling her. 'Which is a good thing.'

They settled Bonny into the shower and Meg completed her handover quietly as Bonny closed her eyes with relief as the warm water cascaded over her stomach. 'Bonny had progressed to eight centimetres dilated when Dr Kefes came in half an hour ago.' Meg stopped as the next contraction hit.

'We've negotiated a short time off the monitoring from Dr Kefes just so she can move around a bit before the birth, but we have to head back to bed as soon as she feels any urge to push.'

Lucy had to agree. 'With twins that's understandable.' The two midwives grinned at each other. It could be tricky balancing two babies and eight people in the bathroom.

Twenty minutes later Bonny looked up with a startled expression on her face. 'It's time.' She turned to face Lucy. 'But I don't think I can move.'

Meg blinked and her face paled but Lucy had a little more experience of this and knew what to do. She leant in and turned off the shower. 'I know. But it's safer for your babies if you do, so we're going to move anyway. Okay?'

She put her hand on Bonny's arm and motioned to Meg to do the same on the other side. 'And I'll buzz so that someone will come and start ringing the troops while we get you back to bed.' She leant across Bonny's body to the wall and pushed the call button. 'Let's go.'

Meg's eyes widened in relief as Bonny stood up and suddenly took off nearly at a run for the other room so that the midwives were almost left behind. She climbed up onto the bed as if she was being chased and by the time Flora arrived they were drying her off and slipping on her open-backed gown.

By the time Nick arrived and Bonny was giving her first push, the foetal monitor was back in place and two baby hearts were making clopping noises.

Nick saw Lucy as soon as he entered the room and forced himself to ignore her.

For some reason, today she distracted him and he wondered if it was because he didn't want to think of Lucy as the patient in a few months' time. The twin thing. He focused on where he should be. 'How are you doing, Bonny?'

'Business end.' Brief and to the point, Bonny wasn't wasting energy on small talk.

Nick nodded and headed over to the basin with a small smile and washed his hands. While he pulled on his gloves, he looked across at Meg and raised his eyebrows in a silent request for an update. Meg was fiddling with the foetal monitor and Lucy stepped in and filled in the blanks, so he couldn't ignore her.

'Bonny went to the shower and about five minutes ago felt the first urge to push. She's had three pushes since then and both foetal hearts have been reassuring.'

Good. Another woman brief and to the point. He liked that. He nodded and snapped his second glove into place.

Bonny groaned as the next powerful urge took over and when they lifted the sheet a tiny dark head of hair slowly appeared like magic between her legs. He stepped in next to the bed. 'You're doing an amazing job, Bonny. Nice and gentle.'

Nick glanced at Lucy. 'Get the paeds, thank you.'

Lucy nodded, sped over to the phone and passed the message to the neonatal staff. A few seconds later she put down the receiver. 'They're on their way.'

At that moment Cade and Callie and two experienced neonatal nurses slipped unobtrusively into the room and he nodded. Not that he expected trouble but he wanted to be prepared for it.

Bonny groaned again, and he looked back at his patient.

Women never failed to amaze him with their strength in these situations. He couldn't help just one quick glance at Lucy, who was holding Bonny's hand as they all waited for the birth. In the not-too-distant future he'd be here to see Lucy give birth.

Lucy watched Nick's large capable hands as they supported the first baby's head as it lifted and turned. She didn't think she would ever forget this moment.

The room calmed as a tiny shoulder appeared, Nick murmuring praise as Bonny silently and unhurriedly eased her baby out. The first of the twins had arrived safely to a sigh of relief from in the room.

Cade stepped up next to Lucy, not saying anything, but she could feel the concentration he was directing her way as Nick passed baby one up to his mother. Lucy rubbed the little body dry until the baby grimaced and then made no bones about complaining loudly.

Bonny's firstborn son screwed up his little face until he was bright red and roared his disapproval and he kicked his legs, exposing his impressive scrotum and penis to everyone except his mother.

Lucy felt Dr Coleman step back and she had to admire his unobtrusive readiness. Maybe he wasn't so bad after all, because he'd certainly achieved what he needed with very little impact on Bonny's birth experience.

Lucy liked that. A lot.

One of the neonatal nurses replaced him and helped Lucy settle the baby between his mother's breasts, mouth and neck nicely positioned for ease of breathing, skin to skin, with a warm bunny rug over them both.

'So what have you got?' Nick smiled at Bonny, because everyone else in the room knew but hadn't said the words.

Lucy lifted the blanket and then the baby's rear end to show his mother, who lifted her head to glance down, and then Bonny laughed. 'A boy. We have our William.'

As they all waited for the next contraction the relief in the room gave way to the tiniest rise in tension. It was always tricky to see how the second twin settled in its mother's uterus after the first had made more room.

Hopefully the baby would turn head first towards the big wide world, but Lucy knew that often second twins would settle into breach position, which was less straightforward for the birth.

What they didn't want was the baby not making a firm decision between the two and lying across the mother's uterus to block the cervix with a shoulder or arm. Such a position became incompatible with a normal birth and Caesarean of the second twin would have to be considered.

'Start the syntocinon, please, Lucy. We want a few more contractions.' Lucy uncapped Bonny's IV cannula and connected the infusion.

Nick's big hands gently palpated Bonny's stomach until he found the hard, circular head of the second twin, who was apparently still undecided on the direction of the exit. Nick kneaded gently downwards along the baby's back through the mother's soft abdomen until the next contraction halted his progress.

After several contractions and Nick's gentle persistence Bonny began to push again.

This time the baby wasn't in so much of a hurry to be born, and the tension crept up until Lucy found herself holding her breath and Nick quietly urged Bonny on.

'Come on, baby,' Bonny muttered. 'If it's a boy, he's called Benjamin.'

Finally the baby's hair and then rest of the head was born, and during what seemed an eternity, but which after Lucy's third glance at the clock she knew was only ninety seconds, the flaccid little body of a slightly smaller twin boy was born in a flurry of floppy arms and legs.

'It's Benjamin,' Nick said. 'We'll take this little one over to Dr Richards for a few minutes, Bonny.' Nick cut and clamped the cord and Callie swooped in, dried the limp baby with the warmed towel and then gathered up the tiny scrap in her confident hands to carry him across to the heated resuscitaire.

'He's a bit stunned so he hasn't taken his deeper breaths to start off,' Lucy said quietly in Bonny's ear. 'Needle,' she warned as she gave the injection to help separate the placenta and reduce the risk of bleeding after birth.

She glanced across to where the two neonatologists were working quietly on Bonny's second twin.

The neonatal nurse who'd stayed to observe William began to explain to Bonny what was happening and Lucy's attention was drawn that way, too.

Within thirty seconds the tiny oxygen saturation probe had been taped to Benjamin's tiny hand and they were puffing little bursts of air into his lungs.

From where she stood she could see his heart rate was reading eighty and that wasn't too bad if it crept up over a hundred with the inflation of his lungs.

But that didn't happen. In fact, the heart rate slowed agonisingly and dropped to fifty.

She heard Dr Coleman's comment to Dr Richards. 'So, secondary apnoea. Change from air to oxygen. I'll do the cardiac massage.'

Smoothly Dr Coleman changed position, circled the baby's chest with his big hands and began to compress the little rib cage three times to every breath from the face mask Callie held over the nose and mouth.

They began inflating baby's lungs with more oxygen and immediately his blueness seemed to wash away.

'He needs a little oxygen until he gets the idea of this new breathing business,' Nick said in answer to Bonny's worried look. 'Pinking up now.' He glanced back at the sudden gush of blood that was forming a ruby puddle in the bed.

The placenta came away and Nick passed it swiftly to Meg in a dish. 'Check it's all there because we've got some bleeding.'

'Fundal massage, Lucy.' Lucy leant over and rubbed Bonny's soft belly firmly until the underlying uterus contracted under her hand to slow the bleeding.

Swiftly Nick checked for any trauma that could be contributing to the blood loss while Meg carried the placenta over to the bench and made sure none of the lobes of tissue were missing from the circle. Lucy knew that sometimes lobes or even membranes from the bag of waters left behind could cause bleeding after a birth.

Nick pulled the spare drape from the trolley and tossed it up onto Bonny's belly. 'I'll do the massage now, Lucy, if you draw me up another five units of syntocinon and get two fifty micrograms of ergometerine ready just in case.'

His big hand came in over Lucy's with the drape between them and Lucy stepped back to assemble the drugs. Nick went on, 'I'm afraid your uterus has gone on strike, Bonny. I have to rub it until it contracts and stops the bleeding. Sorry if it's uncomfortable.'

Lucy held up the first drug to check with Nick and he read the name, dose and expiry date out loud. 'Fine. Give it slowly intravenously. Then start the forty units in a new flask of saline in the line.'

Meg was back. 'Placenta looks complete.'

'Good.' He looked over his shoulder at his registrar. 'Simon, put another cannula in, please, and draw some bloods as you do. Repeat coags and full blood count. We already have blood cross-matched if we need it. You can run normal saline through that as a replacement fluid. I think this bleeding is settling now.'

Lucy leaned towards her patient and took her wrist.

Amazingly, Bonny's pulse was only slightly raised. 'You okay, Bonny?' she asked as she strapped the blood-pressure cuff to the woman's arm.

Bonny nodded. 'I'm more worried about my baby.' At that moment a little wail came from the second re-suscitaire. 'But I think he's getting the hang of it.'

Lucy watched the unhurried way Nick moved through the mini-crisis. She tried to estimate the blood loss and decided it would have been around a litre or two pints. 'Blood pressure one ten on sixty, pulse eighty-eight.'

'Thank you,' Nick said to acknowledge he'd heard, he looked at Bonny. 'You lost an amount of blood that would certainly have caused problems for most adults but thankfully you pregnant ladies have mechanisms in place to cope with extra blood loss at birth.'

He smiled reassuringly a Bonny. 'You still look the pink-cheeked and bright-eyed mum we started with, though tomorrow might be a different story.'

He went on quietly, 'Tummies that have carried twins are notorious for being tired after birth, Bonny, but it's all settling now.'

He gestured to the two IV lines now hanging above her. 'Sorry about the two drips but one can come down when we've replaced a little of the fluid you've lost. We'll run this new flask over four hours and see how you're doing then. Might be able to just put a cap over your IV lines after that.'

Bonny nodded. 'I'll forgive you,' she said, and stroked the little body that still lay across her chest. 'I just want Benjamin.'

Nick glanced across at the team, who only needed to observe her baby now. 'I know. He'll be across here as soon as we can.'

By sixty minutes after birth everything had settled. Benjamin, the second twin, spent a little time with oxygen near his face while he lay on his mother, but soon he was sucking as robustly as his brother from his mother's breast. He'd go to the nursery as soon as he'd finished so he could be watched for another hour.

Nick had gone. Meg had gone home. One of the neonatal nurses had stayed to help Lucy with the babies and they'd been weighed—both had come in at just under seven pounds—and the neonatal nurse was in the process of dressing them.

Lucy took Bonny into the shower and helped her freshen up and climb into her pyjamas, all the time alert in case Bonny began to feel faint, but to her relief the new mum just kept going.

It was incredible how reassuring the whole experience had been for her on a personal level, Lucy thought.

Ten minutes later she finally helped Bonny into bed with her two little guys beside her in the twin cot.

The room was peaceful for five minutes until Bonny's husband arrived with their two little girls, and excited pandemonium broke out.

There were squeals, bed-jumping and excited tears as Bonny's husband squeezed his wife tightly in relief that she and the babies were well.

Lucy was still smiling as she walked away with a promise to return in fifteen minutes to make sure the bleeding remained settled and to check that Bonny had survived the onslaught.

Three hours later, after another emergency trip to Theatre, Nick walked down the corridor to his rooms and deliberately loosened his shoulders.

He was mentally tired but there really wasn't any reason for him to be this drained.

Last night had been torrid in Theatre but ultimately successful.

Today, there had been another good outcome, and he was glad everything had worked out fairly smoothly for Bonny because they'd had many long talks during her pregnancy about her preference for as little intervention if possible. In the end they'd achieved most of that.

But mentally he was distracted, and he didn't do distraction, so where the heck had that come from?

Lucy's worried face at the ultrasound yesterday slipped into his mind. It wasn't a certain little midwife causing all this, he hoped.

He ran his hand through his hair. He guessed he hadn't slept well on Sunday night after Lucy's scare and then they'd been up most of the night after that.

And he'd spent a bit of mind space hoping the scan would come back normal, to the point that he'd made sure he had been there for the appointment yesterday, which, when he thought about it, hadn't really been necessary.

Because Lucy was only a colleague. And a once-only pleasant breakfast companion. And a patient of his. Nothing else.

Not a sister he could put up in his flat until her world righted itself. Not someone he had to go in to bat for when other people let her down. But she was vulnerable and she didn't have anyone else.

Was that why he'd wanted to take her aside after Bonny's birth and make sure she was okay? Maybe give her a hug and reassure her that her own birth would be fine? Her babies would be fine.

This was getting out of hand.

The only ironically amusing part about this was how horrified his parents would have been at his involvement, and how fortunate for Lucy that he didn't speak to them.

He was developing an interest in a non-Greek, pregnant nurse with twins by another man! Well, he knew she was a midwife and not a nurse, but it would be the same to them. Anyone less than a specialist would be a failure to them.

He could hear his mother now. 'This woman, she is after your money. You are a doctor. You are too good for her.'

In fact, he had a sneaking suspicion that Lucy was too good for him. But for some reason she just had to look his way, smile in that cheeky, sexy way of hers, and he was hot. What was that about?

Lust, his inner demon suggested sardonically. He laughed out loud and then glanced around. A hospital orderly dragging a garbage bin looked at him strangely and he pulled himself back under control.

But it was darkly humorous and the joke was on him.

Because lust wasn't going anywhere with a woman pregnant with twins.

Not like he could drag her off to bed for goodness knew how many months so he'd be better casting his gaze elsewhere and scratch that itch with a woman who understood that he was footloose and fancy-free and staying that way. Plenty of those around.

Somehow it just wasn't an attractive thought. But what was most important was that he keep everything under control.

'Would Dr Kefes please phone Emergency. Dr Kefes, please phone Emergency.'

The page boomed overhead and Nick ducked into the

nearest nurses' station to pick up the phone, actually a little relieved to be called to an emergency. Looked like he was going to miss the squash game with Cade as well.

At eleven that night Lucy pushed open the night exit at the front of the hospital and stepped out into the balmy evening.

She was limp with exhaustion but exhilarated by the way Bonny was managing with her babies, and how well both little boys were.

She'd felt so reassured about how Nick had agreed to less intervention, how calm and wonderful he'd been with Bonny, and if everything went well she was going to have babies like that. With Nick as her carer.

She wanted to ask Flora to be her support person because her senior was certainly taking an interest in her well-being and Lucy didn't really have any other friends she could ask to be with her.

It was all months away but she guessed in another couple of months she'd have to start looking for antenatal classes. And going to those alone, too. She lifted her chin.

A car stirred the warm air as it flew past with its headlights on and she stepped up onto the path towards home.

The bonus of living close to the hospital was that it was quick to walk to and fro, but the disadvantage was that at night it could be a little creepy, heading along a street that comprised of mainly driveways and garages behind big walls.

Another car started up and she waited for the acceleration of sound but unexpectedly this one rolled up beside her and Lucy's heart rate soared.

She stared doggedly ahead and refused to look at the driver. It was even harder not to glance round when the passenger window was wound down, and her heart rate bumped up another notch.

'You're not walking alone at night, are you?'

Nick. She blew out the breath she'd been holding in a long stream. Grrr. 'Hell, Nick! You frightened me half to death.'

'Sorry.' He didn't sound it and her irritation went up another notch. 'Would you like to hop in and I'll run you the rest of the way?'

She could guess what had happened. He'd obviously seen her and decided to go all interfering on her. But now her nerves were shot it would be a horrible walk until she was safely inside her own yard.

So she'd look pretty silly if she said no. Especially when her feet were killing her. But there was no use getting used to it.

He wouldn't be waiting every night so what was so special about tonight? The last thing she needed was to feel let down after every shift because Nick wasn't there to pick her up.

Lucy sighed and opened the door but after she'd climbed in she frowned at him. 'Aren't you going the wrong way?'

The seat felt fabulous as she rested back and took the weight off her feet, and that only made her feel more cross. 'Do you have any idea how bossy you sound?'

'Sorry again.' He didn't sound it and she was glad someone was amused. Not. 'It's the Greek in me,' he said mildly. 'I don't like to see a woman walking alone at night.'

Bully for him. 'It's not my preference, but the Australian in me says get over it and get home.'

'I'm Australian,' he said mildly. 'But I'm also second-generation Greek.'

'Hmm.' As in not my problem, Lucy thought, still grouchy from her fright. 'And this is my house. Thank you for the lift.'

He pulled on the handbrake. 'I'll walk you in.'

'No, thank you.'

Nick tamped down his frustration. He was sorry he'd startled her but he hadn't been able to believe it when he'd seen her head off in the dark. He didn't know why he hadn't thought of it before. He guessed he'd assumed she caught a taxi home or something.

But she was so darned independent he should have known she'd put him on the back foot. He forced himself to relax and smile at her as he leant across to open the door. 'Our first fight.'

She didn't smile back. 'It was fun. Goodnight.' She pushed the door wider and climbed out and he watched her walk to the gate, and hated it that nobody would be there to greet her when she got home.

He thought for a moment she was going to just march away but when she took out her key she looked back. Shook her head and sent him one of those ray-o-sunshine smiles he could live off if he had to.

'Sorry. You scared me.' She shrugged. 'I was cross with myself for being nervy and you copped it. Thank you for the lift.'

He let out his breath. At least she didn't hold grudges, though he'd done nothing wrong by wanting to see she was safe. 'In penance you should have breakfast with me on Sunday.'

She grinned at him. 'Now, that would be a hardship. Love to. But I'm—'

He finished the sentence for her. 'Paying for your-self. Excellent. I'm broke.'

She looked startled for a moment and he patted him-self on the back. It had made her smile again. Keep 'em guessing, good motto. 'I'll pick you up at eight?'

'Eight's perfect. See you then.'

Lucy closed the gate behind her as the automatic lights came on then she heard Nick's car accelerate away.

The night noises surrounded her. The owners had only stayed for two nights and now she was back to being home alone.

CHAPTER EIGHT

ONE OF THE fronds from the palm trees crashed down somewhere along the path near the pool and Lucy jumped at the noise and spun around before her brain recognised the familiar sound.

Her babies wriggled and fluttered and she patted her stomach. 'Sorry, guys.' Leftover nerves from the fright Nick had given her.

For the first two weeks she'd house-sat she'd been sure someone had been outside the house when that had happened, but she could have done without it tonight.

She glanced up at the big house and then frowned at the flicker of unexpected light she could see in the lounge room.

There was a small tinkle of glass and this time she knew it wasn't normal. Her hand edged into her bag and she felt around for her phone as she backed towards the gate.

As soon as she was out of sight of the house she pressed the button for contacts and Nick's name lit up. Without hesitation she pressed his number and he answered it on the second ring.

'Lucy? You okay?'

'I'm coming back out,' she whispered. 'Someone's in the house.'

'I'm on my way and I'll ring the police as I come. Get out into the street and under a streetlight.'

By the time Lucy had crossed the street and hurried away from the driveway Nick's car was roaring up the road towards her, and she'd never been so glad to see anybody.

Nick saw her a hundred yards down the street under a lamppost, her arms wrapped around her belly and shaking.

He screeched to a halt and was out of the car in seconds with his arms wrapped around her and her face buried in his shirt. 'You were quick,' she mumbled into his shirt, and he stroked her hair. Poor Lucy.

'I should have walked you into your house.' His arms tightened. 'I'm so sorry.'

'I said no. And I'm not your responsibility.' She eased back as she looked up at him, chin thrust forward and her eyes showing she was bravely determined not to crack. All the conversations, concern, downright worry and now this scare twisted in his gut.

Maybe that was why he tilted her chin with his finger and murmured against her lips, 'It's sure starting to feel that you should be.' And then he kissed her.

It was intended as a gentle salute, a comfort peck, sympathy even, but that wasn't what it turned into.

As soon as she melted against him he lost it, lost where, why, everything except how much he'd wanted to taste this woman, feel her against him.

Her instant response, to open under him and hotly welcome him in, lit a desire that flicked along his arms, tightened his hold and fanned a deep need he hadn't realised he had. He wanted more. He wanted Lucy. He wanted it all.

Lucy was lost. Nick's mouth against hers was intoxicating, hot, hungry and totally in charge. And she wanted more. Wanted to push the boundaries into the world she'd always wondered about. It wasn't safety she wanted at this moment, it was danger.

Apparently 'lost in a kiss' was the way it went with Nick. Swirling sensation, swirling red colours against her closed eyelids.

It wasn't until he was gently pulling away that she caught on to how lost they'd been.

Nick's arm slid over her shoulder and pulled her against him as he faced the uniformed patrolman that had answered Nick's call.

Lucy came slowly back to the real world.

And Nick's voice. 'I'm sorry, officer.'

Officer? Someone else was here? Real red lights were flashing.

Nick's voice again. 'Yes, it was me who called.'

So they'd been sprung in mid-kiss by the patrol car. Embarrassing. Lucy bit back a giggle, still drunk with the sensation of Nick making no bones about the fact that he desired her. Or maybe he'd just been kissing her for comfort and it had been her hormones that had screamed sex. Either way she was a wanton, bad woman and bad mother—so why was she still smiling?

Nick turned her to face the young man in blue, who didn't meet her eyes. She blushed. 'I'm Lucy Palmer, the house-sitter. Yes. I heard glass breaking and there was a strange light moving in the lounge room.'

The young patrol man nodded. 'So you exited through the rear gate and rang Dr Kefes. Who rang us?'

'That's right. We…' She blushed again. 'We haven't seen anyone leave this way.'

The policeman glanced at her this time with a

slight smile. He raised his eyebrows but refrained from comment.

Nick stepped forward and pointed to the gate.

'This path also leads to the beach. It goes past the house, behind the pool and onto the beach.'

Still stunned by her response, Lucy let Nick take control because she was still a foot or two off the ground. At this moment he could run the show for all she cared. They'd stopped talking and it seemed like they were waiting for her to do something. Both of them looked at her hand holding the keys.

'Do you want me to open the gate?'

'If you give me the keys, we'll deal with this. I'm pretty sure they'll be gone now.'

Lucy handed over the bunch. 'The blue is for the gate, the red for the house, and the green for the gate to the beach,' she told the policeman.

'Would you both wait here for us?'

'We'll be here.' Nick pointed to his vehicle and the policeman nodded and motioned to his men to accompany him onto the property.

Nick and Lucy watched them go and the moment stretched to awkwardness as both tried to think of something, anything, that was not embarrassing to say.

Lucy was the first to give up on that unlikely occurrence. 'I thought I was seeing red lights because you were kissing me.'

Nick blinked and then smiled and soon they were grinning at each other. 'And I heard roaring in my ears, which was probably the patrol car trying to run us down.'

Lucy chewed her lip. 'At least no one from the hospital saw us.'

And then Nick said something she hadn't foreseen.

'Much more of that and we have the reality of finding you a new obstetrician.'

Lucy's stomach dropped and she thought, *No-o-o!* with an internal wail of distress. Nobody would be like Nick. She wanted Nick to look after her. Felt so safe under his care. Maybe it wasn't too late. They could pretend it had never happened. 'It was just the stress of the moment. What about if I promise never to kiss you again?'

Nick winced. She could promise that, could she? Maybe she hadn't felt what he'd felt. 'Actually, I kissed you.' *And I'm not promising anything of the sort.* He didn't know what had happened, but he didn't say it out loud.

So it seemed Lucy wasn't ready to hear anything like that and he wasn't going to rush her, or himself, but things had certainly changed.

Or had the possibility of change. And professionally his judgment could be clouded.

He wasn't ready to say just what it was between them but the chemistry was blatant. He wanted to enjoy more of her company, even if it had to be platonic, and he could not believe he was thinking this. That had to be a first.

But he could see she was upset. How to explain? 'It's becoming a little hard to manage your care with the dispassion that is required.' He winced. That sounded sensible but stuck up.

He took her shoulders and tried not to think about what he was feeling beneath his fingers. 'I'm already second-guessing myself, questioning decisions I don't question with other patients. That's not fair to you or to me.' And that was the truth. Apart from the fact his Hippocratic oath forbade him to have a relationship with a patient and he'd just kissed her. And wanted to do it again.

He dropped his hands. Definitely time to bail out.

Why did she have to look so crushed? But as he should have expected, she lifted her chin and accepted reality. It just took a few seconds, and he was reminded of the way she'd coped the first time he'd seen her in his rooms. No hysteria, no tantrums.

He heard her sigh. 'I think I understand, but I wish you didn't have to.'

He wanted to hug her again. More proof he was doing the right thing. 'I'm doing this because I still want to be here for you, Lucy. You're not losing me. You're just gaining an impartial second person.'

She nodded but he didn't think she was convinced. 'If you were impartial, you could keep looking after me.'

'Sorry. Not impartial.'

She smiled shyly and then chewed her lip. 'Do you want me to find the other doctor?'

No! Definitely not. What if she picked someone useless? Someone like Chloe had had? He'd be a mess. How could he say that diplomatically? 'Not unless you want me to. I have a very good friend, just moved back to Gold Coast City after his wife died, David Donaldson, whose care I think is excellent.'

He'd been Nick's mentor. David was old enough to be Lucy's father, and his own too, for that matter, but he was the best with twins, Nick reassured himself. 'I worked with him in IVF at another hospital and he's very experienced with twin pregnancies.'

'He sounds fine. Thank you.'

The conversation died when the police reappeared. They were carrying a plastic bag with a heavy metal bar in it. 'Seems they jimmied open the back door. You must have disturbed them because they left this behind.' He frowned at Lucy. 'Not sure you should stay the night here, miss, it's a bit of a mess in there, and you being pregnant and all.'

But where would she go? 'I'll be fine. I'll lock up and they wouldn't come back tonight.' She swallowed and stuck her chin out. 'Surely.'

She felt Nick bristle beside her and the officer sighed. 'It's up to you, miss.' But he looked at Nick. What was with that? It had nothing to do with Nick.

It was the other Nick who answered. The one from the hospital. Consultant Kefes. 'You're absolutely right, officer.' She could hear it in his voice. 'We'll arrange somewhere Lucy can stay tonight and sort it out in the morning.'

Lucy's mouth opened but Nick went on, 'Has there been a series of these break-ins?'

The officer nodded. 'Half a dozen over the last week, and some injuries to people who have disturbed them.'

Oh. Lucy's heart plunged. Okay. Not sensible to stay if she wanted to keep her babies safe. But a hotel room was going to hurt her budget severely. A wave of tiredness broke over her and she just wanted to go to bed. Somewhere safe.

Nick was shaking hands with the officers and distractedly Lucy thanked them as well.

The policeman shook his head. 'You did the right thing. Pregnant lady like yourself. You hear noises you don't understand and there's someone in the house, you get out, and ring us—any time.' He glanced at Nick. 'We'll respond as quickly as we can.'

'Thank you, officer. We appreciate that.'

Lucy was still trying to decide which hotel would be

the best at this time of night. That was one thing about the Gold Coast. Plenty of hotels. Or maybe she could find a free empty bed in the ward? The man nodded. 'Have a good night.'

They watched the police drive away but all Lucy could think about was how she wanted to sink into the ground. In fact, she wished Nick would go. She had a lot to think about.

Like where to sleep and…that kiss. And how she'd shown him just how much she was attracted to him and the fact that now he just wanted to get her off his books faster than a speeding bullet.

Cringe. Nick's voice broke into her swirling thoughts. 'Come to my flat.'

What? 'I can't do that.' As if.

He opened the passenger-side door of his car. 'Of course you can. It's just sleep. I've got a spare room.'

She couldn't go there. Maybe he could sleep at her place. But she knew he couldn't. Like he could sleep on her two-seater here or in her single bed.

But she couldn't go to his place. 'I can just imagine the gossip.'

'To hell with the gossip. I'm sure a single mother with twins created more gossip last week. And you survived. You can't stay here. It's crazy to pay two hundred dollars for a hotel when you're only going to use it for a few hours. Plus you shouldn't be alone after a scare like that.

'It's for one night.' He glanced at his watch. 'Actually, for about six hours. Are you working the morning shift or the evening?'

'Evening.' So she'd have to come home tomorrow night after work and do the whole thing again. Not an attractive thought.

'Again, problematic.' Nick looked at Lucy wilting under the streetlight. 'It's okay. Just be a little less independent for one night and get in the car.' He gestured to the open car door. 'We'll worry about it in the morning.'

He'd said 'independent' but by his tone he'd meant 'stubborn'. She wasn't being stubborn. Just realistic. It wasn't going to change anything for tomorrow, because this was still her home, but she had to admit it would be horrible to try to sleep at the flat tonight with the trashed house a few feet away.

But she needed to learn to cope with crises as they came along—because she was going to be doing this alone. Nick wouldn't always be there to rescue her.

Nick watched her struggle with the concept of accepting his offer. He wasn't sure either if this was the right thing to do or not, but she couldn't stay here.

She must have been too tired to argue because to his relief she moved past him and slid into the car.

He couldn't stop himself shutting the door quickly in case she changed her mind. He didn't have control issues but the idea of driving away from Lucy while he couldn't be sure she was safe just wasn't happening. He could hear his sister's voice, complaining, the word 'over-protective' ringing in his ears. But this was different.

Tomorrow he'd figure something out. He was good at that. He could fix this. Protect Lucy. Now that she was finally letting him do the work.

CHAPTER NINE

'WHAT FLOOR ARE you on?' Ten minutes later they were standing in the basement car park of Nick's units, waiting for the lift to arrive.

'Nine. It's got a great view.' Nick looked disgustedly relaxed about bringing back a strange woman to his flat after midnight. He probably did it all the time, Lucy thought tiredly.

It was like he hadn't even noticed the tension between them in the car, or the fact that she'd been almost glued against the door on her side, as if she could wipe away any thoughts he might have that she was attracted to him. Too late for that, though.

Lucy had her fingers crossed behind her back. Please don't let them meet anybody in the lift.

The place would be crawling with hospital staff on call for emergencies at all hours of the night and she did not need the stress of smiling and pretending everything was normal when her whole world had been rocked on its axis.

Or was she being a little prude to worry about taking just one night's shelter at a friend's house because her own had been compromised?

A friend she'd kissed, though.

She sighed and forced herself to relax a little. She really couldn't help it.

At that moment the lift doors opened and of all the people she didn't want to see was the glammed-up version of the night-duty midwife, Cass. Even more surprising, she was hanging on the arm of Dr Cade Coleman, and they were obviously on their way out somewhere for very late drinks.

Dr Coleman's eyebrows shot up but he didn't say anything except, 'Evening.'

Nick's sardonic 'Evening' back made Lucy wonder bitterly if this passing of ships in the night was a common occurrence in this building. Neither of the girls said anything, and Lucy's embarrassed smile was met by a disbelieving frown as she and Cass passed.

The lift doors shut and Lucy felt like stamping her foot in frustration. Of all people! Grrr. She looked at Nick, thinking *this was his fault*, and was even more incensed to see he had a slight smile on his lips. 'Well, I'm glad someone is amused.'

'Sarcasm, Lucy?' Nick said mildly, and then he draped his arm around her shoulder and hugged her once before he let her go. 'You're having a night from hell, aren't you?'

She was going to say yes, categorically, but then her sense of fair play, the reasonable side that allowed her to get over the disappointments she'd grown up with, remembered how Nick had come to her aid immediately, had worried about her safety and even provided an answer to her immediate dilemma.

She sighed out her frustration, tried another sigh, and felt better for it. Get over what you can't change. What did she care what Cass thought? But she'd tell the world, her inner caution wailed. Not a lot she could do about it now, though.

So it wasn't the worst night ever. Not quite. 'Not the best.' Though one particular part had been incredible, she wasn't going to think about that until she was safely back in her own house. 'But the night could have been a whole lot unhealthier if I hadn't had you to call on.'

The lift stopped and Nick waited for her to leave the lift in front of him. He lowered his voice. 'Number six. And you're welcome.'

Lucy followed the direction of the numbers until she came to the corner flat. Number six. Nick leant in front of her and opened the door with his key then held it to allow her through first.

Down a small hallway and across the huge living room, floor-to-ceiling windows held the eye, with sheer curtains and a narrow balcony that ran round the whole corner of the building and the view beyond. 'Wow.'

'Yep. It's nice. And there're two bedrooms, so you can have the guest room. You've got your own bathroom and there's towels and a robe hanging on the door if you feel like a shower before bed.'

Bed! It sounded divine. Night attire was a minor problem, but he'd said there was a robe. She looked down at her scrubs. She didn't want to sleep in them or she'd look a hundred times worse tomorrow morning when she met the next nemesis in the lift on her way out.

'I should have grabbed some clothes.'

He shrugged. 'I've got a heap of T-shirts. I'll try and find one that's not black.' He grinned at her. 'We'll sort all that out tomorrow'.

He went to his refrigerator and brought her an un-opened bottle of spring water. 'Take that. You're dead on your feet.'

He scooped a folded T-shirt out of a laundry basket of clean clothes that was sitting on a chair, handed it to her and kissed the top of her head like she was a five-year-old he'd picked up from school. 'And I'll see you in the morning.' And then he left her.

Just walked into his room and shut the door.

Lucy blinked. Well, that had been easy. And bizarrely disappointing, which was ridiculous. But he was right about one thing. She *was* dead on her feet and she could worry about everything else in the morning.

Nick had to get out of the room. Or he would have drawn her into his arms again and who knew where that could have ended? Scary stuff.

He heard her bedroom door shut and a few minutes later the sound of the shower. He tried really hard not to think of Lucy naked, round and glistening, with the water running over the places he wanted to run his hands.

He decided a shower was a great idea because he was damn sure there wasn't much chance of sleep just yet.

The cold water helped and as he dried himself he knew he did need to hit the sack. He had a late start tomorrow but the day would be a long one. Especially if he hung around until Lucy finished work. There was plenty he could do in his office.

They had to sort somewhere safe for her to go. Or she could stay here.

He was getting way too involved in her life but she was like a freight train heading for disaster. Not that she'd see it that way.

After a brief, glorious shower, where she rinsed out her underwear, wrung them dry in a towel and hung them up for the morning, Lucy pulled the T-shirt over her head and tried to ignore the fact she was naked under something that had been against Nick's skin.

A slow heat started in her belly and she couldn't help thinking about Nick's arrival under the lamppost, and the kiss.

She was pretty sure he'd just meant to comfort her but she'd melted against him like a candle under a blow-torch. She would have been a puddle if he hadn't held her up.

She'd never been kissed like that. Nowhere near it. Had never lost herself until all she could feel was a need for more. Her face heated at the thought. And wanted more.

Maybe she'd just been scared? She'd been so glad to see him, and to be wrapped in his arms and protected by him had seemed the most natural thing in the world. Her babies shifted and wriggled and she patted them gently as her head hit the pillow. 'He's not your daddy. And he's not going to be. So get used to it.'

Suddenly there were tears on her pillow and her throat felt raw. She sniffed. 'Stop it.' She rolled over and after many determined breaths and tight closing of her eyes she did eventually fall asleep.

But her dreams were not so easily controlled. Someone was following her. Every time she stopped, they stopped.

When she turned round she couldn't see who they were but she knew they were there and she couldn't find the gate to get out of the house courtyard. Every path seemed to lead to a bare piece of fence with no opening and they were getting closer.

Suddenly she started to cry. She never cried. But the tears just fell more heavily.

A sob caught in her throat and she tried to hold back the flood because the stalker would hear her. Unconsciously she pulled her pillow over her face to muffle the sounds and cried as if her heart would break.

Across the lounge room Nick thought he heard something. Was that Lucy, talking to someone? He slipped from his bed and opened his door.

Nothing. No sounds. Then it came again. Very soft but audible out here. It was Lucy. Sobbing, and nothing could have stopped him knocking briefly and crossing the room to her.

'Shh.' He brushed the hair from her face but she just turned away. 'Lucy, wake up.' He shook her gently but she just became more agitated.

He couldn't stand it. He didn't know what to do except slip in beside her and pull her against his chest and cradle her in his arms. Nick wrapped himself around her until she buried her nose in his chest. He'd never let anything happen to Lucy.

Her hair was in his face. Her forehead in his chest. Babies up against his belly. Now, that was a new experience and he couldn't help a tiny smile.

'It's okay.' He stroked her back. 'My poor brave girl. Life just keeps throwing stuff at you.' He smoothed her hair. She mumbled something he couldn't make out. 'You're fine. You're safe.'

Slowly her breathing settled, and when Nick kissed the top of her head and then her cheek, still with her eyes shut she turned her damp face towards him.

He kissed her mouth gently and she smiled sleepily. 'Go to sleep. I've got you.'

She murmured something and rolled in his arms so she was facing the other way, spooned into him. Nick swallowed uncomfortably. Exquisite agony to lie there with her so trusting against him.

His hand rested as if it belonged in the gorgeous hollow between her breasts and the other splayed on top of her rounded tummy. She snuggled in even closer and he stifled a groan. If it had been anyone else but Lucy he'd have said they were deliberately teasing him.

He felt the first roll of her belly and then a clear kick from one of the little people inside, and he couldn't help but grin.

'Hello, there,' he whispered barely audibly, and the little foot or hand poked at him again.

Warm feelings expanded in his chest. Affection for these little scamps. These wriggling little babies who would have their mother's characteristics.

And their father's! They weren't his babies.

The thought crashed in on him and for the first time he felt the loss of not being a father. Not having the right to cradle a woman's belly and know that he had created a life—or two—within her. The loss stung unexpectedly. Especially with Lucy in his arms. And yet the man responsible wasn't here, and he was.

Nick wondered what sort of father he would have been. Would he have found it easy or hard to relate to his children? Maybe he would be no better than his own intolerant father, but even at this moment he knew that wasn't true. Especially if he had someone like Lucy to guide him.

The babies kicked again and Lucy murmured something. He smoothed the T-shirt-covered belly under his hand. 'Hey, don't wake your mother up.' And he knew he cared far too much about these tiny little girls or boys and had already invested in their future.

Was he just indulging the over-protective nurturing tendencies he'd carried since Chloe had been sixteen?

Tendencies that had been amplified by his profession? He'd always thought he had an inbuilt reservation about commitment. So where had that gone?

He was a fool. Had he invested his heart in Lucy?

Sure, she wanted him to look after her, but she also had no problem saying she'd never kiss him back again if he didn't pass her on to David. Not exactly the relationship he was looking for.

Unconsciously he tightened his hold and she murmured in protest. He loosened his hands and backed away. He needed to get a grip—and not on her. She seemed settled now and maybe it was time to go.

He slipped slowly backwards out of the bed and apart from a small disappointed noise she let him leave. An omen? He pushed his pillow into her back and tucked her in.

Definitely the most sensible thing to do anyway.

Lucy had the best dream.

When she woke up she was smiling despite the shaft of sunlight on her cheek and a baby playing trampoline on her bladder. And the smell of coffee.

Lucy stretched and admitted grudgingly to herself that it had been the best sleep she'd had for months. She slid out of bed and padded across to her bathroom.

After she'd indulged herself with another quick shower and climbed awkwardly into her now dry underwear, she looked at the scrubs and screwed up her nose.

Soon she would change back into a purple Teletubby but not yet. She lifted the thick white towelling robe from the hook on the door and slid her arms into the sleeves. She'd always wanted to walk around in one of these.

She grinned at herself in the mirror, surprised how light her spirits were considering everything that had happened the night before, but maybe that was because she couldn't do anything about all the disasters now anyway.

She tied the belt over her definitely growing belly, and opened the door.

Nick was in the kitchen, breaking eggs into a pan. He was wearing board shorts and a black singlet top.

She swallowed the 'Wow' that hovered in her throat and coughed. 'Morning.' Tore her gaze away and admired the way he added four little rashers of bacon to the pan.

He pointed to the coffee plunger on the bench. 'Good morning. Decaf, my lady?'

The heavenly scent. Oh, yes, please. She looked at him. There was something different about him this morning but she couldn't put her finger on what it was.

She poured herself a coffee and sipped the aromatic brew before she put the cup down and pointed her finger at him. 'You, Dr Kefes, are a prince.' She could squirm and beat herself up over being here or she could just enjoy this and to hell with the ramifications. No choice really.

'And I can even cook.' He smiled a long, slow smile that fitted right into the particularly gorgeous day outside and the incredible aromas inside. Life could not get any better at this moment.

'You look rested. And back to your incredibly serene self.'

She felt great. 'I am. This is a very nice hotel. Your bed is divine and comes with delicious dreams.' She could feel herself blush and went on hurriedly, 'Your shower is glorious.' She twirled and showed off her robe. 'And this is very trendy.'

He took his time admiring her robe. Or he might have been avoiding her eyes. She wasn't sure which.

'Sadly, they don't come in black, apparently.'

'Well, I'm not sad about that.' She picked up her cup and wandered over to the window with maybe a tiny hint of extra wiggle.

Nick must have pulled back the curtains when he'd got up because the unobstructed view of the ocean was breathtaking and there was even a cruise liner out on the horizon.

To the left the balcony looked over the Gold Coast city skyline. 'Wow.' She glanced back at him. 'It must be hard to leave this and go to work in the mornings.'

'Nope. Love my work.' He concentrated on turning the eggs without breaking them. 'Love my life.' The toast popped up and he tossed the slices onto the waiting plates with a whistle.

And let that be a warning to you, Lucy, she told herself sternly. He wasn't looking for a relationship any more than she was, let alone one that came with twin babies and commitments. And she had a very busy life to plan and some serious juggling to make ends meet. Hence the reason she was not moving out of the cabana.

But she wasn't going to let it spoil the short time she had before she dived back into reality.

'Good on you. I love my job, too.' She moved towards the long table set with two places. 'And where do I sit?'

He gestured vaguely. 'Either or. I don't eat here enough to have a favourite chair.'

'But you had bacon and eggs in the fridge in case?' Lucy raised her brows.

He shrugged. 'Mrs Jones does my shopping and laundry as well the flat. She keeps me stocked.'

Cleaning lady. Bliss. This was a five-star resort. 'Fine. I'll take the chair facing the view.'

So will I, Nick thought, and could barely take his eyes off her. Obviously she didn't remember the nightmare or the fact that he'd gone in to lie with her until she settled. In the harsh light of day that was a good thing.

He sat down at the table opposite Lucy and watched her tuck into her food, like she had that time they'd eaten together at the surf club, and it was surprising how much he'd enjoyed cooking for her. He enjoyed having her in his home.

And he wanted her in his bed. He'd lain awake for hours last night. Of course she'd had nightmares. It had been a shock and she could have easily been attacked. He'd spent a fair while beating himself up for not taking her all the way to her door or he would have been there when she'd been first frightened.

Which brought them to the next dilemma, but he let her finish her breakfast in peace before he brought that up. If he knew Lucy, it wouldn't take long for her to polish her food off.

Or disagree with his suggestion.

He could feel a smile tug at the corners of his mouth as she put her fork and knife together in the middle of her empty plate. 'Wow. That was good. Thank you.' Typically she followed that with, 'And I'm washing up.'

She just couldn't let him do anything for her without paying for it. Stubborn woman. He didn't know why that pushed his buttons but he almost ground his teeth in frustration. Maybe that was the reason he was less than diplomatic with his next wording.

'It's not safe to go back there after work tonight. You know that, don't you?'

He frowned at himself. But she was so darned independent she infuriated him. That wasn't to say after it came out of his mouth he didn't regret his bluntness.

She put her cup down and met his gaze steadily. Surprisingly even-tempered as she gently turned him down. Why did he feel like she was the grown-up here?

'I appreciate your concern, Nick, but I have to go back. It's my home. And my job to house-sit the big house.' She held his gaze. 'I need to save money for when I can't work, and it's rent-free.'

He would not lose this battle. 'And what if the burglars come back?' It seriously worried him and he couldn't believe it didn't worry her either.

Lucy sighed. 'The thought of getting home late at night and opening my door isn't a comfortable one, I admit, but I'll have a chat to Flora at work today and see if she can swap me to day shifts for a few weeks.'

He opened his mouth but she held up her hand. Bossy little thing. It had been years since someone had held up their hand to tell him to be quiet. He subsided reluctantly but stewed about it.

'I'll phone the owners this morning when I go home and see what the damage is. I'm sure they'll be happy to beef up the security and maybe even hire a firm to keep the place under surveillance. It's in their interests, too.'

He could see she was determined. But so was he. 'If you work this evening, before you can change to the day shift, I think you should spend one more night here.'

She opened her mouth and sardonically he held up his own hand.

She narrowed her eyes at him but he just smiled. 'My

turn. Another day or two will give the security firm time to make their adjustments as well.'

It was a sensible idea—and, though Lucy hated to admit it, it was an attractive one as well. And that was without the eye candy of a dreamy Greek doc cooking her breakfast. And in reality there was plenty of room here for the two of them.

It would only be for one more night. And the idea of not having to go back until the place was made more secure was very attractive. Maybe he'd let her pay...

'And if you offer to pay board I will stomp on your scrubs so that when you leave, everyone will think you slept in them.'

She widened her eyes at him. 'Ooh. Nasty.'

He wasn't fazed. 'I assure you. I can be.'

'Okay. Okay.' She had a sudden vision of Nick jumping up and down on her purple scrubs and bit her lip to stop an unseemly snort. But it seemed there was no stopping the eruption of giggles that escaped. She gave up and threw back her head and laughed at him.

'You crack me up.'

'Obviously.' He grinned at her. 'Now, that has to be good for you.' Nick was thinking that it was good for him, too. He loved the way she laughed. Loved a lot of things about Lucy because she continued to amaze him with her resilience.

'So you'll stay tonight?'

She nodded. 'Yes, please.'

'I'll walk you home. I've got a backlog of work so I'll meet you in the doctors' car park after eleven.'

'No.' She shook her head. 'It's two hundred yards across a road. Doesn't your sister walk home after an evening shift?'

Yes, she did, but this was a bit different. Or was it?

Was he going too far the other way? What was wrong with him?

Hmm. 'You're right.' He held up his hands. 'My brain's gone AWOL.' He stood up, walked over to an empty vase and tipped it up to retrieve a spare set of keys.

'The big one opens the door on the street to the foyer. The smaller one the front door to the flat.'

She looked at the keys in his hand and reluctance shone out of her worried eyes. 'I'll try and be quiet when I come in.'

'I sleep through anything,' he said to make her feel better, but he knew he wouldn't.

CHAPTER TEN

LUCY FELT THE change as soon as she walked into work.
The morning staff, normally chatty and warm, suddenly
stopped their conversations when she entered the tea
room, and even the friendliest midwives, while they
still smiled a greeting, didn't meet her eyes.

Lucy took one guess at what had happened. Cass.

She put her bag away and went back out to the ward
to wait for the clinical handover to start.

She'd thought she'd got over that insecurity thing
left over from her mother, that not-good-enough-to-be-
included cloud that had hung over her whole childhood.

So what if these people she'd hoped were her friends
thought that, because she was pregnant, she'd shacked
up with the nearest available rich guy and had just made
it easy for herself?

Now she wished she'd actually tried to seduce Nick
so at least she would have had the memory. And what
a memory that would have been...or would she have
been just like her mother? Looking for a quick fix to
her life's bigger problems?

Then they'd have the right to say she'd be a terrible
mother, too, but she knew in her heart that wasn't true.
She would love her babies with all her heart. Though

there would always be a part of her that belonged to Nick in her dreams.

Lucy lifted her chin. She'd always been a bit of a loner when the going got tough. Other people didn't need to know how she was feeling so she pinned a smile on her face and put her bag away.

But the unfairness burned a hole in her euphoric feeling of belonging here. How would they have liked a break-in? At eleven at night? When they were on their own?

All they saw was the pregnant little midwife who might be sleeping with the ward consultant. A man who wasn't even the father of her baby. Or maybe they thought Nick was.

Poor Nick. His only fault was that he'd helped her out. Well, blow the lot of them.

Flora appeared at her side. 'A moment, Palmer?'

Lucy felt her stomach plummet. She'd thought Flora would have given her the benefit of the doubt. 'Certainly, Sister.'

Flora steered her into her office and shut the door. Then, to Lucy's complete surprise, offered one of her jerky and uncomfortable hugs before she pulled back and stared into Lucy's face with concern. Not censure. 'Are you all right?'

Dear, dear, Flora May. Lucy stamped fiercely on the urge to cry. 'My landlord's house was broken into last night and I disturbed the robbers when I went home.'

Flora gasped.

It all tumbled out. 'Nick came and phoned the police and waited with me. He thought it wasn't safe to stay alone in the flat.'

'He's right.' Flora looked away and glared into the

distance. 'Stupid rumours. Stupid people.' Flora looked back at her.

Now seemed a good time to mention the roster change, Lucy thought. 'I was going to ask if you could change me to day shifts for a few weeks. I spoke to the owners today. A security firm has put the house under surveillance but I'd like to avoid going home at night for a little while.'

Flora nodded vehemently. 'Absolutely. Consider it done. You could have night shift if you wanted. Then you'd only be there in the daytime.'

But then she'd have to work with Cass and they just might come to blows if she still treated her birthing women like she'd treated young Sally. Or Lucy herself. 'Can I think about that?'

Flora nodded. 'No problem. Why don't you have split days off this week? Have tomorrow off and come in Friday and Saturday morning because I have a space on the roster then.'

Flora stepped back to the desk and checked her print-out. 'Yes. Then have Sunday off then do a week of mornings starting Monday?'

Sounded perfect. Lucy wondered if Nick still wanted to have breakfast together on Sunday—he might be sick of her by then after having her in his house for two days in a row—but either way she still wasn't working. Flora was a champion.

She did have friends. 'That sounds wonderful. Thank you.'

Flora glanced at her watch. 'Let me know if you want nights next week.' Then she looked back at Lucy's face. 'And where are you going tonight after work?'

'Um, Dr Kefes has offered his spare room for one more night.' Flora didn't look happy and Lucy went on,

'The new locks and cameras at my place will be installed tomorrow. So tomorrow night I'll go back there.'

'Fine. I'll have a word with a certain midwife.'

Lucy shrugged. 'It really doesn't matter. I should be used to it.'

Flora lifted her chin. 'You shouldn't have to be. But I will fix her little red wagon.' Goodness knew what that meant, Lucy thought, but she wouldn't like to be on the end of Flora's displeasure.

'Oh. And Dr Kefes said because it could be misconstrued, he's moved me on to a Dr David Donaldson. Do you know him?'

Lucy hadn't known that Flora could actually blush, though there was a definite heightened colour to her face.

The older woman seemed fixated on the ward clock now. 'Yes. I heard he was coming back.'

Lucy wasn't sure what the problem was, but she hoped it wasn't because Flora didn't agree he was the right doctor for her. 'Apparently his wife died.'

'Hmm.' Flora wasn't buying into the conversation. 'You don't see your mother much, do you? Did you ask her to come and stay with you?'

Lucy shrugged. Would her mother offer her help if she needed it? She really didn't want to find that out the hard way. 'She's got her own life. I respect that. And my flat's too small for two people.'

Flora nodded noncommittally. 'I have my own life, too, but I'd like to think that if you need a friend I am there for you, Lucy.' It seemed a strange thing to say and not related to anything.

Lucy mumbled, 'Thank you,' and the subject closed on that.

'Take birthing unit two,' Flora said. 'Judy is in there and will give you handover.'

Eight hours later, as the shift drew to a close, Lucy couldn't help the little release of excitement that had bubbled quietly all day because she'd be going back to Nick's flat again tonight. And everyone already thought they were having an affair.

But this was the last time she'd stay there. It had to be.

Tomorrow, a Thursday off for a change, she'd have all day to sort things out and be ready to sleep in her own bed tomorrow night. She needed to get back to running her own life.

A shame it had felt so safe at Nick's flat last night. As if the weight of the world had been lifted off her shoulders and this morning had been the perfect way to start the day. The picture of Nick, with his muscles, in the kitchen, cooking her breakfast, would be hard to beat.

As Lucy turned towards the consultants' flats she hoped she wouldn't meet anyone in Nick's lift this time but it probably didn't matter now. She was already the scarlet woman of the hospital, just like her mother, heading to sleep over at a man's flat.

Not such a good example to her children, and something she'd sworn when they were peanuts she wouldn't do, but this was different. How far she'd fallen since that first exciting day when she was going to be the best grad midwife GCCH had ever seen.

Lucy's hope that tonight's stay at Nick's would remain unnoticed shrivelled and died as the nurse walking ahead turned into the front entrance to Nick's lobby door.

Not much she could do about it unless she wanted to walk around the block in the dark, and that defeated the purpose of being safe, she thought grumpily. She rubbed the tender ache in her side where one of the babies had been poking her with an elbow or foot on and off throughout the day.

As she opened the foyer door a few seconds later with Nick's key she could see the other nurse was still waiting by the lifts so she'd even have to say hello.

She sighed and admired the thick loose twist of dark hair on the woman's head and even the escaping brown curls looked more artful than untidy. She'd always wanted to be able to do a bun.

Lucy brushed back the hair from her own eyes and felt hot and bothered and frumpy and fat. Where had all that excitement of five minutes ago gone?

Quite a few years older than Lucy, the other girl offered a friendly smile. 'Evening.' And Lucy wished for half her poise.

'Evening.' Lucy decided that must be what they all say around here and the conversation died because the lift doors opened.

'What floor?' the girl asked as she stood in front of the control panel.

'Nine.'

The girl's brow puckered a little and she glanced at Lucy more thoroughly as she pressed the button. 'I'm on nine, too. Haven't seen you before.'

Lucy studied the shiny white tiles of the lift floor. 'I'm just staying with a friend for tonight.'

'Oh.'

Lucy looked up at the change in tone. She saw the other girl digest her answer as she looked at Lucy's baggy scrubs and the unmistakable bulge of pregnancy at the front. Her eyes narrowed.

The tone wasn't unfriendly. 'I'm Chloe Kefes.'

Bingo. She had all the luck. 'Nick's sister.' Lucy tried to keep the resignation out of her voice.

'Yep.' Her gaze was drawn to Lucy's bulge. 'Would you be Lucy? His patient?' Chloe had a twinkle in her eyes that took the sting out of her next comment. 'The one the whole hospital is talking about with my brother?'

At least Nick's sister didn't seem to hate her. 'That would be me. And ex-patient. Actually, he's handed me over to Dr Donaldson.'

Chloe's eyes widened. 'I see. Good. I'd hate him to have to justify to people what he does naturally. He's the kindest man in the world and the best brother.' She raised her eyebrows at Lucy. 'Gets a bit over-protective at times.'

The lift arrived and Lucy had never been so glad to step out. 'I know. And I do understand. Nice meeting you, Chloe.'

'Interesting meeting you, too.' They walked down the corridor together and Lucy remembered Nick pointing out his sister's flat next to his. This just kept getting better and better.

Chloe's eyebrows rose when Lucy pulled the key to Nick's door out of her pocket but she didn't say anything. Before Lucy could turn the key Nick opened the door anyway.

'Hi, Lucy, Chloe.' He looked from one woman to the other. 'Did you guys walk home together? That's a good idea.'

Chloe looked like she might disagree but didn't comment. 'We met in the lifts. I'll see you in the morning, Nikolai. Bye, Lucy.'

Nick held the door for Lucy and she closed her eyes as she ducked under his arm. This was becoming more complicated by the second. She should have just gone back to her own home. She'd tidied up the big house before work today and maybe she would have been fine.

'I don't think your sister is happy I'm staying.'

'Tough.' He looked supremely uninterested. 'I'd be more unhappy if you didn't. Who matters most?'

She had to smile at that. 'I guess she's worried the gossip will taint you.'

He looked more closely at her. 'Have you had a bad day or was it just Chloe?'

She sighed and allowed herself to be steered into a chair. He handed her a soda water and she took a sip because she hated the way, even without intention, Chloe had made her feel. 'I'm a scarlet woman, having an affair with the consultant.'

He shrugged and then smiled crookedly at her. 'I hope I'm the consultant concerned?'

'Stop it.' But he did make her smile despite the gravity of the situation. Not that he seemed to think it grave.

He sat down opposite her. Caught and held her gaze. 'You're new here. You're not used to it. The place thrives on gossip. Next week it will be someone else.'

'I don't want to be this week's juicy titbit.'

Nick couldn't stand it. She looked so forlorn. Juicy titbit. She was that indeed, but at the moment she needed comfort, not his sexual frustration, and he'd promised himself he would not sleep with Lucy.

It wouldn't be fair. What single, pregnant young woman, after giving herself, wouldn't be hurt when he walked away?

And he wasn't capable of the emotional roller-coaster ride needed to stay. He owed it to her to be strong for both of them.

So gently, like a brother, he stood, reached down and

she put her hand in his without hesitating, and he held that thought as he stood her up. 'In that case, come here and get a sympathetic hug.'

Before she could pull away he'd folded her loosely in an embrace and just for a moment he felt her let the worries and stresses fall away. But only for a moment. Would she ever let him in? he thought ruefully, forgetting he'd agreed on keeping his distance, not thinking about his own walls that held them back.

A few more seconds and he'd have to let go. She felt too good, snuggled in against him, too rounded and lush and gorgeous. Maybe they should really give the gossipers something to moan about.

Lucy relaxed against Nick and tried to stop thinking. Just for a moment. Then she remembered the safe harbour last night, remembered the time he'd hugged her when she'd been frightened for her babies, remembered he'd kissed her once. She didn't want this for comfort, she wanted it because he desired her. Because all night while she'd waited for the clock to crawl around she'd hoped he'd do this, because she certainly desired him.

She just wanted him to sweep her up, show her the love she had no right to expect, because she had the horrible feeling she was reading too much into his kindness. Learning to rely on him too much. And he had a real life apart from being her shiny white knight in her fantasy.

She didn't kid herself he'd be dropping by with his paddleboard when she had two tiny babies to manage. What man would?

So she'd be the one doing the moaning if she let herself snuggle up to Nick for too long. She shouldn't have come here tonight feeling needy and emotional, and more than semi-sexually aroused at the thought of sleeping under Nick's roof again. She'd heard that the second half of pregnancy hormones could startle men. She smiled sadly to herself and prepared to ease back.

But she never got to take that step away because Nick lifted her chin with one long, caring finger, smiled into her eyes and kissed her. A soft and sweet and gentle kiss.

It was too much. Lucy despaired. The tragedy of this beautiful, too-perfect man, and the chance of him falling for her, nearly broke her heart. Something must have shown in her face because he gathered her even closer, whispered, 'Don't look like that, my gorgeous girl,' and kissed her again.

And then it was just like last night, under the street-light, a long star-studded, sensation-filled path to losing herself in a place where no rational thought was allowed.

'Hold me, Nick.' She didn't know where the voice had come from, or even if she'd said it out loud, but she felt the floor disappear from under her feet as he lifted her into his arms and carried her carefully into his moonlit room.

Nick put her down gently on her feet beside the bed, murmured, 'Far too many clothes,' and helped her pull off her purple scrubs so that she stood before him in her bra and panties. Then he pulled his T-shirt off and drew her back in against his chest. Skin to skin. Like a baby against its mother's breast. Her lace-covered breasts against Nick's chest.

She could stand like this for ever—his hot skin on hers, lean muscle against her soft curves. She pictured them in her mind's eye to save the memory, inhaled the scent of freshly showered man, leant into solid, muscular chest, lifted her hands to corded shoulders and slid her fingers along the rough growth of his un-shaven chin.

Every part of him felt as wonderful as she knew it would and her body began to dance to his music as his hands slid slowly from her shoulders to her hips.

He made her feel wanton, desirable, for a moment even beautiful, and she tilted her head as he dropped feather-light kisses along her jaw.

She'd dreamt of this but it had never felt as magical as this.

Emboldened, her hands began their own exploration, the play of muscle and sinew and raw strength under her fingers, the bulge of biceps, and with a woman's smile she felt his breath catch as her thumb slid across his taut belly.

The sliding doors to the veranda were open and the sound of the surf washed over them as he drew her down gently onto his bed and with her eyes shut by his kisses, the soothing sound of the waves and the salty freshness of the breeze surrounded her, along with Nick's arms as he lay down next to her—and pulled her more fully into his embrace.

When he kissed her again she sighed into him. This was where she wanted to be. She had been fighting against the dream, fighting against the taboos of falling for a man who wouldn't be there for her always, but it was too late. She loved him for what he'd done for her, loved him for looking after her babies, loved him even when he undermined her independence, even loved it that he was so confused about his own feelings for her—but that didn't mean he loved her.

I love you, she said silently to him, and hugged him tighter because she needed this one night before she returned to the real world tomorrow.

* * *

He hadn't meant to get to this point. he held Lucy in his arms and she felt so right, so perfect that it scared him. Terrified him that this woman—his hands slid with gentle reverence across her satin belly—and these babies—his breath caught—could be his responsibility.

But was he ready for this? Did she think he was? Was he open enough emotionally, worthy? Could he be trusted to never let them down, like his parents had let Chloe and himself down? He hoped so but hope wasn't good enough. In his heart he knew that 'not sure' was unacceptable.

But still he couldn't stop because she pulled his hand back when he tried to leave, answered when he kissed her mouth with a molten response that undid his intentions, pressed herself against him until his need for her outstripped his brain's refusal.

But this couldn't happen while he wasn't committed. He owed Lucy that.

So, after a timeless journey of sensation, intoxicating kisses and the tender wonder of this woman's beautiful body, Nick drew back. Shuddered the demons back into their boxes and stilled his hand.

Lucy sensed the change. In some pathetic part of her a tiny molecule was glad that one of them had stopped because this had no future and she would hate Nick to regret it.

It was fortunate indeed that Nick had more control than she did.

But, then, he didn't love her.

He probably cared for her and was happy to be there when she was having one of her many crises, but for now he soothed her disappointed murmurings with, 'It's okay. We'll talk in the morning. Sleep and I'll hold you.'

And she felt like weeping as he gently rolled her onto her side until they were spooned together, slid his arm beneath her pillow and then cradled her breast in one hand and her belly in the other. And she sighed away the longing, acknowledged in some recess of her brain this was how it would always have ended, and that when she woke tomorrow this book would close.

For ever. Because she couldn't open herself to this kind of pain again.

Lucy closed her staring eyes with the unpalatable insight that Nick was being kind and unintentionally she'd asked too much of him.

It took Nick hours to go to sleep. Apart from his screaming frustration as he held her gorgeous body against him, it was the generous innocence of her response that tore at him. The innocence testified to her pre-pregnancy inexperience and how low he'd been to even consider making love to this woman without a full commitment.

She was so different from the other women he'd been with. He hadn't understood, hadn't learnt what Lucy's kind of giving was about, so maybe he could cut himself some slack that he hadn't recognised what he was doing until almost too late.

But it had opened a deep well of wonder, and also great guilt.

He needed to rethink this whole Lucy world. Because that's what she was. A world. An amazing, generous, loving world that he wasn't sure he was ready for. Or deserved. He fell asleep wishing to hell he did.

When Nick finally fell asleep it was so deep he

didn't feel Lucy rise before the sun. Or hear the blinds being drawn across to darken the room from the pre-dawn light before she slipped away. Or the rustle as she dressed herself in the lounge room with the new clothes she'd picked up yesterday. Or the sound of his front door closing as she carried everything she'd brought with her back to her own house.

Lucy knew she needed to go. Preferably before Nick woke up because, unless she wanted to be the Nikolai Kefes groupie of the year, she had to get out.

She wasn't sure if this was a final stab at the inde-pendence she needed to survive or the ultimate in self-protection. All she knew was that her babies deserved more respect and she needed more self-respect than the morning after an almost-affair from a man who had only ever been kind to her.

And most terrifying of all, she needed to go before Nick trapped himself into something she refused to see him regret.

Even before Nick woke up his hand searched for the warmth of Lucy. His eyes opened but the dent in the pil-low beside his head only made him feel sad. He strained to hear the sound of movement in his flat but all he could hear was the relentless ocean, washing in and washing out across a deserted beach, and in his heart he knew she was gone.

He couldn't believe how empty, and deserted, his own life seemed, so different from yesterday when he'd bounded out of bed to make her a surprise breakfast. Today—it was just him. Like old times.

Times before Lucy. He couldn't believe how much he missed her.

Nick rolled out of bed, walked to the blinds and pulled them back. He wished he could share the sunrise with Lucy because she'd have enthused over it. He wished he could have seen her bathed by the golden light.

An ominous prickle under his skin asked the question. What if she never came back? If he never woke to Lucy beside him, ever?

He searched for a note but didn't find one. He resisted the urge to phone her. Had to give her space she'd silently asked for by leaving and take on board that it was time to sort out his own issues before he saw her again.

Tomorrow morning. At work. He could wait till then.

CHAPTER ELEVEN

LUCY TRIED SO hard not to think about Nick. About leaving his bed in the early hours like a thief.

But he was the thief. He'd stolen her heart and nobody was going to get it back for her so she needed to grow another one. And that wasn't going to happen unless she stayed away from Dr Kefes.

But it was so hard to pretend she didn't miss him. When she swept the path, she thought of Nick, and got hotter than she should. When she picked a frond out of the pool her stomach dropped as she thought of Nick. Opening her refrigerator even the water bottles reminded her of Nick.

But the worst, when she lay on her bed, she missed his warmth. His strength. His caring.

Could even hear him telling her to stay, the day he'd run all those errands for her, when she'd been scared she'd lose her babies. But she had to be strong.

For both of them. For all of them.

On Friday morning, Flora introduced Lucy to Dr Donaldson on his first day back at GCCH. He was a tall, smiling, stick figure of a man with very kind eyes, so it seemed strange, when Nick had endorsed the man to her, that Flora obviously wasn't comfortable with him.

Lucy's first antenatal visit with the new doctor was that afternoon after work. It had been arranged by Nick on Wednesday, with strict instructions not to miss it, and while she'd been steamrollered into changing doctors, it seemed now it was all for the best.

The shift was busy, but thankfully Flora was still allocating her non-Kefes patients. Lucy saw Nick twice in the distance, but ducked into a room each time before he saw her, and once she turned round when he'd started to walk towards her.

All painful, heart-wrenching choices she had to make, and at times she wasn't so sure she was doing the right thing. She had to face him some time but she was feeling too fragile yet.

Flora seemed preoccupied, and Lucy, hunting for distraction from thoughts of Nick, tried vainly for an opportunity to broach the subject of why she didn't like Dr Donaldson. If she wasn't having Nick, she wanted someone good.

Finally, at the end of the day as both were about to leave, Lucy caught up with the senior midwife. 'As far as Dr Donaldson is concerned, do you think he's a good obstetrician?'

'Of course.' Flora seemed a bit short, and Lucy still didn't feel any better.

I'm not reassured, Lucy thought, and tried again. 'Would you recommend anyone else?'

Flora stopped walking and sighed. She met Lucy's worried eyes with a strange expression on her face. 'David Donaldson is an excellent obstetrician. Very experienced with twin pregnancies and has a stellar reputation. You could do no better.'

Well, that was glowing, it just hadn't been said in an enthusiastic voice. But at least Flora wouldn't say something that wasn't true. And there was no doubt Flora would prefer it if Lucy dropped the subject.

So, reluctantly, she did. 'Thank you.'

Fifteen minutes later she was shown into the good doctor's new rooms and Lucy suspected that behind the twinkling grey eyes lay a very astute mind because he glossed over the point that Nick had handed her on for personal reasons and concentrated on her pregnancy.

After taking her blood pressure and weight, he helped her climb up onto the examination couch to feel her tummy. It just wasn't the same as doing this with Nick but she needed to stop thinking about that.

Dr Donaldson palpated the babies, and he must have been a little firmer with his hands than Nick because once or twice Lucy winced with discomfort.

He lifted his hands. 'Sorry. So you're twenty-four weeks, the babies are growing well, one is head first and the other breech today.'

She nodded. Wished she could tell Nick that one was breech at the moment.

The kind doctor smiled. 'You know they can swap and change for a few weeks yet?'

After he'd found and listened to their two different heartbeats he wiped off the gel and palpated one more time on the lower part of her abdomen.

Lucy winced again and he nodded to himself. 'I thought that was uncomfortable?'

She nodded and he quizzed her on her general condition. 'So you're well. No discomfort you didn't expect, babies moving as usual. Anything worrying you?'

Did he mean apart from tearing herself away from the man she wanted to spend the rest of her life with? She'd barely thought about her body—too obsessed with pining for Nick. 'Just a few aches and pains. But probably ligament discomfort or a mobile elbow.'

Dr Donaldson was more interested than she was. 'Show me where.'

Lucy pointed to the right side of her abdomen, the spot that he'd touched, and he nodded, and gently palpated the area again.

Lucy winced and his eyebrows drew together. 'Haven't had any temperatures? Sweats? Nausea?'

Well, actually… Hot and feeling sick? Lucy nodded reluctantly. 'Yes. I might have.'

He smiled kindly and helped her sit up. 'One or all three?'

To be honest? 'All three?'

He helped her down from the couch and directed her back to the chair beside his desk.

But she'd just thought the day was warmer than expected, the babies were growing and making themselves known, and the stress of moving back into her house, away from Nick, was making her feel a little rotten.

He sat back behind his desk and typed on the computer. 'I'd like you to go down to Pathology and have another blood test.'

Not again. But she wasn't having any unusual tightening of her belly. 'I've already been treated for a kidney infection.'

He smiled. 'I think it's more likely you have a grumbling appendicitis. Fairly unusual in pregnancy and quite complicated with twins on board, but we'll keep an eye on you.'

Lucy felt her mind go blank. Appendicitis? Where was Nick at this moment? What would he say about this? So it wasn't a baby elbow or knee. And it was still a bit achy from where he'd palpated. She couldn't afford a grumbling appendix. 'What happens if it gets worse?'

He smiled kindly. 'You have an appendectomy.'

Good grief. Why did this have to happen today? When she was being strong about not calling Nick? 'I didn't think I could have a general anaesthetic. What about the babies?'

Let alone the six weeks off work with no sick pay. And she wouldn't even have Nick to bring her healthy yoghurt and sympathise.

'Yes is the short answer. If necessary, your babies would be anesthetised as well, because the drugs do cross the placenta.'

Too scary to even think about.

'The babies would wake up when it wore off.'

This was a nightmare. And a hundred times worse because she couldn't share it with the one person she wanted to.

She needed him. But she couldn't have him. 'Don't tell Dr Kefes.' The words were wrenched out of her and were the direct opposite of what she really wanted. More than anything she wanted Nick with her. More than anything she knew she couldn't. This was the start of it. She had to push him out of her life.

This was her surviving the next crisis without Nick.

She'd already had two disasters he'd had to manage and she needed to sort this herself. The problem was, all she felt like doing was bursting into tears.

'You remind me of someone I used to know.' Dr Donaldson gave her a quizzical look. 'Determined to be independent. But I won't mention it if you wish. And your symptoms might go away. We can hope.'

He gave her his card and wrote his mobile phone number on the back of it. 'So take it gently. Phone me if there is a problem or the pain becomes severe. You must do that.'

She nodded, took the card and put it in her purse.

He opened his door for her and before she walked through he said gently, 'And don't forget to have that blood test done today.'

She stopped. Looked at him. He smiled blandly. Surely Nick hadn't told him she'd done that last time? She narrowed her eyes at him. She'd bet Nick had mentioned it. 'Thank you, Doctor.'

Nick found himself wondering how Lucy had gone with Dr Donaldson.

He'd woken so many times on Thursday night, wondering how she'd gone back to her house after the break-in. How she'd gone after leaving his bed. Was she thanking him for not seducing her or hating him? The jury was still out how he felt about that himself.

His eyes strayed to the clock again. She'd be in there now. He knew he'd miss Lucy but he hadn't realised how much he would miss his frequent interaction with Lucy's babies when he handed her on. And this was only the first visit. It was worrying how invested he'd become in her babies' well-being.

He'd been subtly trying to catch their mother's eye all day, without drawing the attention of the whole hospital, watching for developments, but it had been frustratingly difficult to even get close to speaking with Lucy.

He hated the distance he could feel between them and that was despite the fact he was ten rooms away. In the end he'd asked Flora how she'd gone at home, an innocent question, and had been told she was fine.

He'd have it out with her on Sunday, when they had breakfast, if she was still going to come with him. He didn't like to think how much he had riding on the assumption she would.

On Saturday morning Lucy felt well enough to work the early shift, despite the fact she'd been miserable all night, missing Nick, because the discomfort in her side remained constant but was no worse.

After work Flora was coming around late afternoon with some baby clothes and that was something she could look forward to. She needed more distraction like this if she was going to stay sane.

Baby clothes. She hadn't had a chance to do anything yet but her friends with their twins had promised to bring a load of things around next weekend. Lucy decided to ask Flora to come when they did and they could all have an afternoon together.

More distractions and moments to look forward to. Funny how her friends were all older now.

Her midwifery training friends were all far flung and busy partying. Finding herself pregnant on her first shift had made her less outgoing with her mind more on survival than on forming friendships.

Except with Nick. Always her thoughts came back to Nick.

He'd taken her under his wing from the first day. But you couldn't be a pseudo sister when you fancied the big brother so she was doing the right thing to get out of that situation as soon as possible. Before he did.

Everything else was fine. Truly.

She wouldn't be as lonely when she'd had the babies, went to play groups and met other mums. But for the moment it was brutally lonely and not just because she missed Nick. Mostly that, but not only that. She just needed to keep reminding herself.

By the time she finished work at three she didn't feel quite so well.

At four o'clock, when Flora arrived with her freshly baked scones, Lucy was feeling pretty darned miserable.

Flora took one look at her and made her sit down. 'What's happening here?'

Lucy felt like crying. Or being sick. Or both. 'Dr Donaldson thinks I might have a grumbling appendix.'

Flora felt her forehead. 'Hot! It looks to be more than grumbling. You need to go to Emergency, my girl.'

'Dr Donaldson gave me a number to ring him on if I got worse.' Lucy pointed to her handbag on the table. She didn't have the energy to get up and get it herself.

Flora picked up the handbag and brought it over. She dug out Lucy's purse and gave it to her. 'And you haven't?'

Another urge to weep. 'I didn't like to bother him on a Saturday.'

Flora patted Lucy's shoulder and stood up. 'I'll pack you an overnight bag. What about Dr Kefes? Nikolai? Have you told him you're unwell?'

Lucy felt so miserable. And hearing Flora say it only made it worse. 'I'm trying not to lean on Nick. He's treating me like his little sister. It's not fair on him and I have to learn to stand on my own feet...' She put her face in her hands and squeezed her eyes to hold back the tears. She was pathetic.

'Hmph,' Flora said as she stood up. 'I don't think it's a sister he wants.' Flora spoke more to herself than to Lucy as she bustled around. 'And you are a very capable young woman so stop beating yourself up. Shall I ring him?'

Nick would take control again. And she'd throw herself on his chest. She knew she would. She needed to learn to rely on herself. 'No. Don't bother him.'

Flora sighed as she busily rummaged through Lucy's drawers. She held up a soft nightgown. 'This one okay? These underclothes?'

Lucy sniffed and had to smile. 'Nobody has ever packed a bag for me before.'

Flora glanced at her. 'Maybe it's time you let them.'

'Let you?' Lucy would have liked to laugh but she didn't have one in her. 'Could I stop you?'

'I doubt it.' Flora came back to Lucy and leant down, all elbows and awkwardness, and hugged her. 'Stop worrying about putting other people out. They wouldn't help if they didn't want to. Now, do you have a small bathroom bag?'

The pain was getting worse. 'No. I've never needed one. But my toothbrush is there.'

'Never mind. I'll put it in a plastic bag and bring you one later.' She stopped for a moment and sighed again. 'Give me David's card and I'll ring him.'

It all happened very fast after that.

Flora drove her to the hospital, a scary trip in Flora's big off-road vehicle, and with Flora's attitude that everyone needed to get out of her way because she had a medical crisis.

Lucy wanted Nick. Needed Nick to hold her hand. Say her babies would be fine after the anaesthetic. But it was too late now.

The emergency staff knew she was coming, Dr Donaldson was waiting, and before she knew it she was repeating her name to the gowned theatre nurse as she was being wheeled into the operating theatre.

When she came round, it felt like she'd been stabbed.

Der, she had been, she thought groggily, and then she remembered her babies.

Her hand slid gingerly across her belly for reassurance and there they were. Probably asleep, like she wanted to be, and she glanced at the empty chair beside the bed and tried not to cry before she drifted off again.

Flora had arranged for Lucy to be cared for in the maternity section, and that meant she knew the people who cared for her. Except Nick didn't come.

In her groggy haze they all seemed genuinely concerned for her and maybe she wasn't quite as friendless as she'd assumed. Even Cass apologised for not knowing about the break-in, and her less-than-flattering comments that had caused the gossip storm.

Lucy brushed it away. She really didn't care any more but Cass apologised again when she brought Lucy jelly for breakfast before she went off. Lucy just wanted Nick but she knew she couldn't have him.

Down the road from the hospital Nick had gone round to Lucy's at eight o'clock as arranged for Sunday breakfast, but the gate had been locked and when he'd used the intercom she hadn't answered.

Late Saturday afternoon, when he'd got home from a function he'd promised Chloe he'd go to, he'd tried to confirm their date for today and just hear her say she was settled. But that hadn't happened.

He hadn't rung later, even though he'd wanted to, in case she was sleeping. He knew she was due to work yesterday to make up for the Thursday, that would be Thursday when she'd left his bed, but he pushed that thought away.

And he'd rung this morning but there had been no

answer and now she wasn't answering the intercom. He didn't like that one bit.

He'd told himself she was probably doing something industrious around the mansion but this time when he phoned and it again went through to the message bank his skin crawled at the thought of Lucy unconscious or, worse, attacked by criminals in her own home.

Why on earth had he agreed she should come back here when he knew it wasn't safe? Three nights she'd been here alone.

Nick strode the long way round and peered over the rear beach fence but again he couldn't see any movement. He called out but there was still no answer and now he was seriously concerned.

It wasn't easy but he managed to scale the gate without impaling himself on the protective spikes. He could just imagine the headlines in the Gold Coast newspaper if he did. *Well-known obstetrician impaled during break-in.* Lovely.

No doubt Lucy would have a giggle about that one. After he'd strangled her for scaring him.

And no doubt the security firm would be haring to the rescue by the time he got to Lucy's cabana. They'd better be, he thought grimly, or heads would roll.

When he reached Lucy's flat it was locked up. It seemed she wasn't lying on the floor unconscious from what he could see through the white curtains and the place didn't look as if it had been rifled.

He heard a car screech to a halt outside and the sound of the gate. At least that was slightly satisfying.

Maybe she'd just forgotten their meeting. Not good for his ego or his heart, but better than the alternative.

'Stop right there.' The burly security guard stood with his feet planted as soon as he got inside the gate.

Nick decided that attack was the best form of defence. 'Do you know where Miss Palmer is?'

Belligerent eyebrows shot up. 'And who might you be to her?'

Good question. What was he? He wasn't her doctor. He wasn't the father of her children. He certainly wasn't her brother or her father. 'I'm a concerned friend.' Certainly not her boyfriend—why was that? Because he didn't know his own mind!

It was becoming clearer by the second.

'Prove it.' The man's tone suggested he'd been lied to by experts in the past.

Nick didn't have time for this. He needed to find Lucy. 'I'm Dr Nikolai Kefes. I work at Gold Coast City Hospital.' He pulled his business card from his wallet. 'I want to know she's all right. I was here the other night when her house was broken into and she's supposed to meet me for breakfast today.'

The security guard took his card. Nodded. 'I can understand that, sir. But you will have to leave unless I get Miss Palmer's permission for you to stay.'

'As it seems neither of us knows the answer to her whereabouts I'll be leaving anyway.'

The man nodded. He stepped aside so that Nick had to leave first. At least the security seemed to be working, he thought.

The only other person who might know anything was Flora May. He'd try her first and then the police.

Flora answered on the first ring.

'Lucy is in hospital.'

Nick couldn't believe what he was hearing. 'She's where?'

'In Maternity, post-appendectomy.'

A sudden surge of anger took Nick by surprise and

he forced himself to hold back the explosion he would love to have unleashed. It wasn't Flora's fault. Or only a small part of it. She could have rung him. Finally he managed, 'The babies?'

'Seem fine. No sign of prem labour. Lucy is still very sore and a bit dopey from the pain relief but she's fine, too.'

He was still having problems comprehending that he'd been excluded. 'Why didn't someone phone me? Why didn't you? Or David? I can't believe this.' After all he'd done. All the other crises he'd helped with.

There was a pause. 'She asked us not to.'

Nick couldn't believe that Lucy had deliberately excluded him. Had his friendship to her not meant anything? 'She what?'

Flora paused again. Reluctant. 'I'm sorry, Nick. She said she didn't want to bother you.'

The words chilled him. Iced his veins in a way he hadn't expected. 'Bother me?' Her precious independence. It hurt so much that he wanted to smash something. He thought of the state-of-the-art twin stroller he'd been looking at. All the times he'd been there for her. God, he was such a fool.

'Fine. Thank you.'

'Nick.' Flora at her most urgent. 'Listen. She's young, doesn't want to lose her independence, is used to looking after herself. She's not good at taking.'

This was about that all right. 'I know all about her independence, Flora. She can have it.' He would have been there for her. All she'd had to do was ask. Or include him when she told the rest of the world.

'Nick?'

'Gotta go. See you Monday.' Not that he was looking

forward to that. Lucy would still be in hospital and he
was hurting so much he didn't think he could talk to her.

Lucy didn't know what was wrong with her. Post-
operative blues perhaps. She'd slept all night and
through Sunday morning, her tummy was okay, the
babies were waking up, and she had a beautiful vase
of spring flowers from the staff. But she missed Nick.

She'd sort of thought he would have found out and
visited by now. Maybe she should have asked Flora to
ring him but it all seemed a bit needy now that everything was over.

Flora bustled in, on her day off, and brought a bottle
of apple juice and a pretty glass instead of the usual foam
cups to drink out of. 'My. Don't you look miserable.'

'Well, thanks for that.' Lucy stifled a weak laugh
because even that hurt, and Flora looked contrite. 'No.
You're right.' She guessed Flora knew that she and Nick
were more than friends but less than anything else. You
never knew what crossed the line with Flora.

'Um. Has anyone mentioned to Nick that I'm here?'

'He rang me this morning.'

Lucy had the feeling Flora was choosing her words
carefully and her stomach sank. 'It would be fair to say
he's upset we didn't inform him earlier.'

'Oh.'

Flora sat down and pulled her chair closer to the bed.
'I think you hurt him, Lucy. He was very—I was going
to say upset, but I think angry and confused might be
better words. And it's not something I've noticed before with our Dr Kefes.'

Lucy said, 'Oh,' again, in an even smaller voice, and
wanted to hide under the pillow. 'I just didn't want to
bother him.'

Flora sighed. 'So I told him. I think that upset him more.'

She pleaded with Flora but inside she knew really she was pleading to Nick. 'I don't want to be a nuisance. He's been so good to me. And I can't expect him to look after me.'

'Oh, don't I know that feeling,' Flora said softly, then she pointed her finger at Lucy. 'And why not? I got the impression he enjoyed looking after you.'

Lucy looked anywhere but at Flora. 'Because he has his own life. He won't want to be saddled with a silly young midwife who got herself pregnant with twins by another man.'

Flora snorted. She did it every well. 'You underestimate your attraction. Women do that. Why do you think he helped you? Allowed you to stay at his flat? Went to the trouble to hand you over as his patient?'

Lucy looked at Flora but maybe she had misread Nick's interest. 'Because he's kind? And I needed help?'

Flora shook her head. 'You have an inferiority complex. Not his problem if he didn't care. But he made it so.' She patted her hand. 'Do you remember me saying people wouldn't help if they didn't want to?'

Lucy nodded. Maybe she had been too prickly. Too determined she wouldn't be needy. Had too jealously guarded her independence and her ability to be hurt again by someone she loved.

'From what you told me, you did a lot for yourself growing up. I understand that. I'm not saying you should use people but you aren't very good at taking help from others. You might want to cultivate that skill.' She laughed. 'Especially with twins coming.'

Then Flora said something startling. 'Did I tell you I was an orphan?'

Lucy shook her head. Looked at this strong, power-ful woman and tried to imagine her lost in a dormitory with motherless children. It was a heart-rending picture.

'Had to look after myself in the orphanage. I was the same as you. So when I grew up I found it very dif-ficult to allow others to try to shoulder some respon-sibility for me. To the extent that eventually nobody tried any more.'

Flora chewed her lip. 'I lost a good man because I wouldn't let him in. He married someone else and I joined the army. Don't make the same mistakes I did.'

She squeezed Lucy's hand. 'Now I'll leave you to rest.'

Suddenly Lucy wondered, and maybe it was the loose-tongued side-effect of the pain relief or maybe her own emotional state but she blurted out the question before she put thought into it. 'Was it Dr Donaldson?'

Flora pursed her lips and didn't say anything for a moment. Then her eyes twinkled. 'Could have been. And I have learnt my lesson.'

She narrowed her eyes at Lucy. 'So you need to learn yours.' Then she stood up. 'Now, let's get you tidy and I'll fix your hair.'

When his sister knocked on his door after work on Sun-day and Nick answered it, he saw her eyes widen at the sweat that poured off him, and he couldn't have cared less.

'I'm about to have a shower.'

'Good.'

Nick didn't need this. He'd run about twenty kilome-tres and he needed to sit down. 'Not in the mood, Chloe.

'So I see.' Chloe pushed a curl behind her ear. 'Just

thought you might want to know that your little friend had an emergency appendectomy last night.'

He grunted. 'I know.'

'Okay.' Chloe paused but Nick didn't offer anything else. She shrugged. 'Thought you might. Just checking.'

Nick wanted to shut the door but maybe he had been neglecting his sister lately for a certain someone who didn't want his attention. 'You okay?'

'Better than you, I think. Let me know if you want to talk, Nicky. It would be nice to be the one leant on for a change, instead of me relying on you.'

After his shower he felt better. And after fluids and food he felt almost normal. Much better for him than the bacon and eggs he would have had this morning. Which brought him back to this morning.

He'd really lost it when he'd realised he'd been excluded from Lucy's emergency.

He wanted to see Lucy. See for himself that she was okay. That her babies were okay. But now he didn't know if he could open himself up to offering her more support if she was going to turn him down.

He needed to re-evaluate his priorities. See his way to the woman he was beginning to think he needed more than he needed anything else in his life.

Should he talk to Chloe before he talked to Lucy? Because this was way outside his experience.

He didn't even know if he could do that. Be the one who needed help instead of the other way around.

Chloe opened her door and she shook her head. 'I don't believe it.'

'You said to come.' But now he wanted to leave. She

must have known because she put out her hand and took his wrist. Pulled it.

'Sorry. You took me by surprise. Come in.' And she drew him into her flat and sat him down.

Nick wondered what on earth he was doing here. His sister was looking at him like he had something terminal and he wasn't used to being on this side of the fence—not being the one who sorted out the chaos.

'Nicky, you're a mess.' She shook her head. 'It's about Lucy. Isn't it?'

He looked across the room at the sea outside the windows. 'I lost it this morning.'

'You never lose it.' He could hear the surprise in his sister's voice and there was a certain irony in that. There'd been times when he'd been close to losing it while he'd been trying to make ends meet as he'd waited for Chloe to grow up.

He shrugged. 'She told them not to ring me when she was sick. I would have been there for her. Why would she do that?'

He could read her sympathy. He didn't want pity. He wanted answers.

'I don't know.'

He knew it. Chloe had no more idea than he did.

When she said, 'Why do *you* think she did that?' he knew it was no good. He wasn't any good at asking for help.

He stood up and Chloe shook her head. 'I've never seen you like this, Nikolai.'

He hesitated and finally sat down again. Ran his hands through his hair. 'I've never felt like this before.'

'Lucky you,' his sister said dryly. 'And poor you.' Chloe chewed her lip. 'So you've slept with her.'

Nearly. 'I didn't sleep with her.' Well, he had but that was all. He didn't get the response he expected.

Chloe looked at him like she didn't know who he was. 'Why on earth not? I thought you fancied her. And I'm pretty sure she's in love with you.'

'Of course I fancy her but she's having twins, for goodness' sake. And I needed to get my head around where we were going.'

'You're allowed to have sex when you're pregnant, Nicky.' Chloe shook her head. 'You knocked her back and she left.' Chloe looked out the window herself and thought about it. 'I'd have slipped away while you were asleep.'

He blinked. 'She did.'

'After a knock back like that I wouldn't talk to you again.'

How did she know this stuff? 'She hasn't. She's moved back home. Avoided me.'

'She's decided to go noble.' She looked at him. 'Your Lucy is a good woman, Nicky. But I'm not surprised she told them not to ring you now she knows you don't love her. She doesn't want to trap you into something you don't want.'

What was Chloe talking about? 'But I do.'

'Do what? Give me specifics!' Chloe wasn't letting him off without him saying it.

'Love her. Want her.' He thought about that. Repeated the words in his mind. Of course he knew that. What the hell was wrong with him? 'But she's so darned independent.'

Chloe laughed. 'But isn't that what draws you to her? You can't control her. Isn't that one of the things you secretly love about her? Why she's worth fighting for?'

He stood up. Hell. Of course it was. And of course

he'd never said he loved her. He needed to do that. 'Wish me luck.'

Chloe hugged him. 'Of course I do.'

CHAPTER TWELVE

WHEN NIKOLAI ARRIVED at the hospital he didn't go straight to see Lucy. Running on instinct, he saw Flora May leave Lucy's room and followed her back to the lifts.

Flora turned when she heard him behind her. She smiled. 'So you came anyway.'

Nick shrugged and smiled ruefully. 'Wasn't going to.'

Flora sighed. 'It can be an awkward and difficult game.'

Nick knew what she was talking about. He wondered how long she'd known he was smitten. 'What game would that be?'

'Don't play with me, Nikolai. She's miserable. She's in love with you. Has no idea you're thinking long term.' She tilted her angular face at him and pinned him with a direct look.

'That is what you're thinking, isn't it?' Flora huffed. 'Because if you're not…'

Nick grinned. He liked this woman more and more, and Lucy could do worse when she looked for champions.

'Yes.' He held up his hands in smiling defence. 'I want to be there for Lucy. And for her babies. For ever.' He shrugged and the liberation of just saying that out loud, hearing those words leave his mouth, filled him with a feeling of marvellous resolution. This truly was where he was meant to be.

'She makes me smile just watching her. I love everything about her, maybe even her independent streak, which, I guess, I'll just have to get used to it.'

Flora laughed. 'Afraid so.'

'I love her you know.' He shook his head. 'Besotted and I didn't realise it.'

Flora said again, 'It's not always a smooth journey.'

Nick straightened. 'Now all I need is someone to ask for her hand.'

Flora's face softened and she patted his shoulder. 'Have my blessing. You're a good man. And a lucky man. And Lucy is the one you need to ask. I just don't know if our Lucy has even allowed herself to dream there could be a happily ever after.'

She stepped back and pushed the lift button. 'She's just had more pain relief. You should go and fix that misconception before she falls asleep.'

When Nick entered Lucy's room she had her eyes closed and her red hair was plaited neatly at the side of her face. He remembered Lucy saying she couldn't do a good plait, had never been taught, and he bet Flora May had done that before she'd left.

He put the single red rose down beside her bed on the chest of drawers and sat down. He'd watched her sleeping before.

She was frowning in her sleep and he worried, with a pang, if she had pain. He hadn't been here and she must have been scared when they'd told her she needed to have the operation.

'I should have called you,' she whispered, and he saw that she was awake.

He leant over and kissed her forehead. 'Yes. You should have.'

'I missed you. I'm sorry I didn't call you.' Her eyes glittered with unshed tears and his heart squeezed because she was upset.

'I'll let you off with it this time but don't do it again.'

She smiled sleepily. 'I only have one appendix.'

He smiled. She was so cute. 'I'm sure you'll find a new ailment some time in the next four months. And if you don't, there's always labour.'

Her eyes clouded. 'But you're not my doctor. You won't be there with me in labour now.'

He took her hand and held it between his. 'I'd very much like to be there with you if you'll have me. And I was thinking of a more legally binding arrangement than being your obstetrician.'

She frowned and he could see the drug was starting to work well.

'I'd like to be with you whenever I can.' He leant over and kissed her on the lips this time. Very gently. 'Go to sleep. I'll sit here and we'll talk about that when you wake up.'

When Lucy woke up Nikolai was still there. It hadn't been a dream. And as for the things he'd said before she'd gone to sleep, she hoped she hadn't dreamed that. He was playing with a single red rose, spinning it in his hand, and she drank in the sight of him until he noticed she'd woken up.

He smiled and the whole room brightened. She loved his smile. 'Hello, sleepyhead.'

Suddenly she felt very shy. Surely this tall and gorgeous man hadn't said what she'd thought he'd said. 'Hello, there.'

He was still smiling. 'How are you feeling?'

Nervous. 'Better.'

'Good.' He nodded and there was that little catch of accent she almost missed now because she was so used to him. Maybe he was nervous, too. The thought brought a little calmness.

He went on. 'And you are properly awake?'

She nodded and moistened her dry lips with her tongue. Nick's eyes darkened and he leaned backwards and picked up her glass of water and a straw from the pile Flora had brought. 'Would you like a sip of water?'

Well, she would, but the suspense was killing her. 'Only if you're quick.'

He passed the water and she took a fast sip before he put it back. He frowned over her words and then got it. Laughed out loud. 'Am I being too slow for you?'

'Maybe a little.'

'Lucy Palmer, I should have told you earlier.'

'Yes.' Lucy wanted to cross her fingers he wasn't going to ask her to be his patient again.

'I love you. With all my heart.' Words she'd never hoped to hear.

Her mouth refused to work. How did you answer that?

His brow creased. 'Is that okay with you?'

More than okay, but she still couldn't speak, so she nodded. 'I love you,' he said again, and she blew him a kiss.

Nick must have seen that as a positive sign because he took her hand and went down on one knee beside her bed. Stared into her eyes with an expression she'd thought she'd never see on his face. 'Lucy Palmer, will you marry me?'

Lucy felt the tears sting her eyes at her gorgeous man, down on one knee, looking into her eyes with the promise of loving her like she'd never been loved before. Fulfilling dreams she'd only dared to dream as she fell asleep in her lonely bed, and here he was, offering her the world. His world.

Waking up with Nick every morning. Sleeping in his arms every night. Her babies would be their babies and if they were blessed they would make more. A family with Nick. How had this happened to her?

Then she said something dumb. 'Are you sure?'

He shook his head. Pretended to frown at her. 'Flora May said you wouldn't believe me. You're supposed to say yes!'

Lucy blinked. 'You've already told Flora?'

'I had to ask someone for your hand.'

She smiled. Loved the idea of Nick asking Flora. Someone else who had really been there for her. Joy bubbled up with the sudden belief that this just might be true. Nick loved her. She loved him so much. Had loved him from the day he'd taken her to breakfast.

'Um, can you ask me, again? Please?'

Nick nodded, suddenly serious, and she loved that, too. Nick serious was Nick seriously sexy.

'Lucy Palmer, I love you. With all my heart. Will you marry me?'

This time she had the right answer. 'Yes. Yes, please.'

He leaned forward and helped her sit up. Then his arms were around her and she felt as if she'd finally come home. Nick's chin on her hair. His arms around her. Home.

She was home with Nick. She'd found her man,

who understood her, loved her and would be her family for ever.

And she would be the home he'd lost at too young an age, the love he could always be sure of. The life he could trust his heart to. She would always be there.

CHAPTER THIRTEEN

LUCY AND NIKOLAI'S wedding took place at sunrise on the beach at Coolongatta an hour south of the Gold Coast, two months after Lucy and Nikolai's twins were born.

As the sun peaked over the ocean horizon the bride walked slowly down the long silver carpet to the edge of the sea where her groom waited with love in his eyes and a swelling so great in his heart he could barely breathe.

Gold and red lights shimmered through her hair as she was blessed by the first rays of the sun, just like their marriage would be, and the trailing wildflowers of her bouquet danced and swayed in her shaking fingers as she closed the gap between them.

He glanced at the assembled guests, seated on white chairs in the sand, more wildflowers edging the silver ribbon that led her to him. To his baby daughters, Phoebe and Rose, being nursed at the moment by Callie Richards for the service.

To the attendants: his best man, David Donaldson, Flora May's new husband; his bridesmaid sister, Chloe, smiling beside Flora May, the Matron of Honour looking tall and gangly with joyful affection in her eyes when she, too, looked back at his bride.

Then his eyes were drawn irresistibly to his beautiful Lucy—the woman who had resurrected his belief in family, given him such joy—and healed his heart. His bride.

Lucy wore a ring of flowers in her hair and her neck rose from the circular neckline of her dress like a swan, and at the hem, her coral-tipped toes peeked out as she walked towards him. He'd always loved her bare toes.

When she put her slender fingers into his he linked her to him and finally believed this dream was real. He'd found the woman he wanted to spend the rest of his life with and he could barely wait to pledge his love, for ever.

* * * * *

Mills & Boon® Hardback

October 2013

ROMANCE

The Greek's Marriage Bargain	Sharon Kendrick
An Enticing Debt to Pay	Annie West
The Playboy of Puerto Banús	Carol Marinelli
Marriage Made of Secrets	Maya Blake
Never Underestimate a Caffarelli	Melanie Milburne
The Divorce Party	Jennifer Hayward
A Hint of Scandal	Tara Pammi
A Façade to Shatter	Lynn Raye Harris
Whose Bed Is It Anyway?	Natalie Anderson
Last Groom Standing	Kimberly Lang
Single Dad's Christmas Miracle	Susan Meier
Snowbound with the Soldier	Jennifer Faye
The Redemption of Rico D'Angelo	Michelle Douglas
The Christmas Baby Surprise	Shirley Jump
Backstage with Her Ex	Louisa George
Blame It on the Champagne	Nina Harrington
Christmas Magic in Heatherdale	Abigail Gordon
The Motherhood Mix-Up	Jennifer Taylor

MEDICAL

Gold Coast Angels: A Doctor's Redemption	Marion Lennox
Gold Coast Angels: Two Tiny Heartbeats	Fiona McArthur
The Secret Between Them	Lucy Clark
Craving Her Rough Diamond Doc	Amalie Berlin

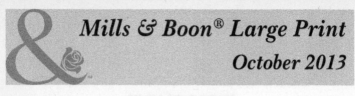

Mills & Boon® Large Print

October 2013

ROMANCE

HISTORICAL

MEDICAL

ROMANCE

Million Dollar Christmas Proposal	Lucy Monroe
A Dangerous Solace	Lucy Ellis
The Consequences of That Night	Jennie Lucas
Secrets of a Powerful Man	Chantelle Shaw
Never Gamble with a Caffarelli	Melanie Milburne
Visconti's Forgotten Heir	Elizabeth Power
A Touch of Temptation	Tara Pammi
A Scandal in the Headlines	Caitlin Crews
What the Bride Didn't Know	Kelly Hunter
Mistletoe Not Required	Anne Oliver
Proposal at the Lazy S Ranch	Patricia Thayer
A Little Bit of Holiday Magic	Melissa McClone
A Cadence Creek Christmas	Donna Alward
Marry Me under the Mistletoe	Rebecca Winters
His Until Midnight	Nikki Logan
The One She Was Warned About	Shoma Narayanan
Her Firefighter Under the Mistletoe	Scarlet Wilson
Christmas Eve Delivery	Connie Cox

MEDICAL

Gold Coast Angels: Bundle of Trouble	Fiona Lowe
Gold Coast Angels: How to Resist Temptation	Amy Andrews
Snowbound with Dr Delectable	Susan Carlisle
Her Real Family Christmas	Kate Hardy

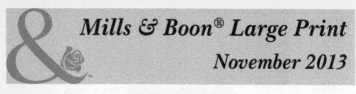

Mills & Boon® Large Print
November 2013

ROMANCE

His Most Exquisite Conquest	Emma Darcy
One Night Heir	Lucy Monroe
His Brand of Passion	Kate Hewitt
The Return of Her Past	Lindsay Armstrong
The Couple who Fooled the World	Maisey Yates
Proof of Their Sin	Dani Collins
In Petrakis's Power	Maggie Cox
A Cowboy To Come Home To	Donna Alward
How to Melt a Frozen Heart	Cara Colter
The Cattleman's Ready-Made Family	Michelle Douglas
What the Paparazzi Didn't See	Nicola Marsh

HISTORICAL

Mistress to the Marquis	Margaret McPhee
A Lady Risks All	Bronwyn Scott
Her Highland Protector	Ann Lethbridge
Lady Isobel's Champion	Carol Townend
No Role for a Gentleman	Gail Whitiker

MEDICAL

NYC Angels: Flirting with Danger	Tina Beckett
NYC Angels: Tempting Nurse Scarlet	Wendy S. Marcus
One Life Changing Moment	Lucy Clark
P.S. You're a Daddy!	Dianne Drake
Return of the Rebel Doctor	Joanna Neil
One Baby Step at a Time	Meredith Webber

 *Mills & Boon® Online*

Discover more romance at
www.millsandboon.co.uk

- **FREE** online reads

- **Books** up to one month before shops

- **Browse our books** before you buy

…and much more!

For exclusive competitions and instant updates:

 Like us on **facebook.com/millsandboon**

 Follow us on **twitter.com/millsandboon**

Join us on **community.millsandboon.co.uk**

Visit us Online   Sign up for our FREE eNewsletter at
www.millsandboon.co.uk